STANDING GROUND

This book is about
where I grew up and
where I work now.

Craig Steven Mullis

STANDING GROUND

Craig Steven Mullenix

TATE PUBLISHING & Enterprises

Published by Tate Publishing & Enterprises, LLC
127 E. Trade Center Terrace | Mustang, Oklahoma 73064 USA
1.888.361.9473 | www.tatepublishing.com

Tate Publishing is committed to excellence in the publishing industry. The company reflects the philosophy established by the founders, based on Psalm 68:11,
"The Lord gave the word and great was the company of those who published it."

Book design copyright © 2011 by Tate Publishing, LLC. All rights reserved.
Cover design by Blake Brasor
Interior design by Kellie Vincent

Published in the United States of America

ISBN: 978-1-61777-556-7
1. Juvenile Fiction, Social Issues, Values & Virtues
2. Juvenile Fiction, School & Education
11.06.03

DEDICATION

In memory of Juan Aguilera and John Castillo, St. Anthony brothers.

ACKNOWLEDGMENTS

There are entirely too many people to thank for the publication of this book. I thank the students in Houston, Texas, that teach me so much on a daily basis. Without them, this book would not have happened and would not have been needed. I thank Karen McConn and Rebecca Hoyt, who both read early versions and took time out of their busy schedules to unselfishly give input. I thank my high school English teacher, Dan Higgins, who, through early encouragement, inspired me to write. I thank Andy Cook, who unknowingly, through his own passion for writing, gave me my first impulse to put the fingers to the keypad. I thank Mr. Bill for supporting me, listening to me, and being more excited than myself at this accomplishment. I also thank Dorothy Allen and Milton

Allen for their ideas. I want to thank Jesus Christ, who inspired these words without my conscious awareness at the time. Thank you all.

"Our children are our future. Let us listen to them, their words, their ideas, their cares, and their frustrations. For it is our children who hold our future in their hands, more so than we hold their future in ours. This book is for all who have hardships and persevere. It is for the poor who overcome. It is for the rich so that they may understand. It is for the students so that they can experience and share. It is for the teachers so that they will open their eyes, hearts, and minds. It is for all, because we all have value, worth, and the possibility of a bright future."

—Craig Steven Mullenix

TABLE OF CONTENTS

VOCABULARY

SPANISH	PRONUNCIATION	ENGLISH
adios	(AH–DEE–**OHS**)	good-bye
barrio	(**BAH**–REE–OH)	neighborhood
comida	(COH–**MEE**–DAH)	food
con	(COHN)	with
fajitas	(FAH–**HEE**–TAHS)	skirt steak
frijoles	(FREE–**HOL**–ES)	beans
gracias	(**GRAH**–SEE–AHS)	thank you
hermanito	(AIR-MA–**NEE**–TOH)	little brother
hola	(**OH**–LA)	hello
huevos	(HOO–**EH**–VOHS)	eggs
mi hijita	(MEE–EE–**HEE**–TA)	my little daughter
mi hijito	(MEE-EE–**HEE**–TOH)	my little son
mi hija	(MEE–**EE**–HA)	my daughter

mi hijo	(MEE–*EE*–HO)	my son
muchos	(*MOO*–CHOHS)	many
niña	(*NEE*–NYA)	little girl
papi	(*PAH*–PEE)	daddy
pobre	(*POH*–BREH)	poor
primas	(*PREE*–MAHS)	girl cousins
quinceañera	(KEEN–SEH–AHN–*YE*–RA)	
		fifteenth birthday
Señora	(SEN–*YOR*–AH)	Mrs./Ma'am
tía	(*TEE*–AH)	aunt
tio	(*TEE*–OH)	uncle

SURPRISE ATTACK

Clarisa grabbed her boyfriend's hand and gave a soft smile. "Thanks, babe. I appreciate you gettin' me a chocolate bar. You know that's my favorite!"

Israel gently rubbed her hand with his thumb. "Hey, no big. Anything for my girl."

The haze of the night made the glow of the bright streetlights unfocused. As they walked to the edge of the busy street, they stretched their necks out and looked down each way of the flat, dimly-lit thoroughfare. In the distance, they saw tiny headlights. They bolted across, hand in hand.

"So we're goin' back to your place, right?" Clarisa always wanted to know the plan.

"Yeah … I guess. Ain't no one there, but we can hang there before you go home."

Suddenly, all too familiar sounds from the neighborhood began.

Crash!

Their heads jerked around to look toward the small convenience store.

"Israel, someone threw something through the window and shattered it!" Clarisa clutched his hand tightly. They saw a couple of bodies scurry out of the doors of the store with their arms full of merchandise.

Surprised, Clarisa stood like a statue and gazed at the robbery. "Did you see that?"

"Yeah, babe, I see. It ain't right robbin' that old man like that. He's cool with everyone."

Suddenly, a shower of rocks and small pebbles flew their way. Instinctively, they darted behind a couple of trees.

Israel's chest swelled and sank as he gasped for air. His heart seemed to be pounding for a way out of his body as sweat trickled down the side of his cheek. A lonely drop clinged to the tip of his nose as he bent over and grabbed his knees, feeling like the world was falling to one side. Clarisa's head throbbed as she heard the thumping of her racing heart in her ears. The musty night air bore a large weight on their shoulders. Smoke from the mufflers of passing cars hit them in the face. Finally, they gathered enough strength and nerve to peek out from behind the trees to see who was standing in front of the store. As Israel wiped his eyes, blurry shadows collected beneath the streetlights in front of them.

"Who are they?" Clarisa whispered?

"Don't know. Can't see real good."

Without warning, a rock buzzed by his ear, crashing through the window of a vacant building behind them. Then another rock flew, smashing into Israel's lower leg.

"Aargh!" he screamed in pain.

"Oh my God, Israel!" Clarisa ran to him.

Israel knelt on the cement and blindly brushed his hand along the ground for something to throw back. His palm found broken glass, causing him to wince as the feeling of warm blood trickled to his fingers. Quickly, he turned and hid behind the tree again.

"Israel, calm down! You're going to hurt yourself more!" Clarisa knelt down next to him and grabbed his hand to look for small shards of glass. "I … I don't see anything too bad here."

"Dang! I'll get 'em! I'll get those punks if it's the last thing I do. I'll get 'em all right! That's for sure," Israel spouted.

Clarisa looked into his fierce eyes. "Israel, calm down."

Israel stood and grabbed Clarisa's arm with his good hand. "Come on! Let's go!"

They darted out from behind the trees and headed into the darkness. Laughter was heard in the distant background as they scampered into the neighborhood.

Israel had not been attacked in the streets for quite some time now, nine months to be exact. He never got scared, not in the streets. But Clarisa realized that these boys had surprised him.

His bloody hand pounded with pain. Suddenly, he felt something cold and wet running down his leg. They both hoped that the injury was not bad. Were they being followed? They kept running for a couple of blocks more until they felt safe enough to stop and examine his injuries. His hand hadn't stopped bleeding, but he knew the cut wasn't deep.

Clarisa held his injured hand close to her eyes. "That looks a little nasty, babe."

"No big. It'll be okay. I've had worse."

Clarisa knew that was true.

The left leg of his jeans was cold and wet, shiny in the moonlight. Grabbing his jeans with shaky fingers, he felt stickiness and smelled a sweet odor.

"Blood?"

As he held up the bag of groceries he had purchased that was supposed to last for the next three days, they noticed the bottle of orange juice was broken, probably shattered by one of the rocks that came his way. Their relief of him not being badly injured was overshadowed by the realization that his meal for the night was ruined. The bread was soaked from the broken juice bottle. Again, hunger would be a familiar friend for a couple of nights. The bottle of soda that made it through the ordeal was little consolation.

"Aw, babe, that was all you had," Clarisa said. "Do you want to come to my house? We got stuff to eat." Her eyes sparkled in the moonlight.

"Naw, that's okay. It'll be all right. I'm not hungry now, anyway."

They walked the rest of the way down the obscure, winding streets until he arrived at the old, cracked front door of his apartment. The door creaked as it wobbled open. Inside was a cave, with darkness and silence their only company. Without turning on a single light, Israel felt his way along the walls toward the kitchen. Clarisa followed closely next to him, gripping his shoulder. Spider-like, his fingers walked across the kitchen table, finding a lone chair. There, he sat down and pulled the soda out of the wet grocery bag. Clarisa perched herself on his lap and began combing through his hair with her fingers. She closed her eyes and gave him a loving hug. Israel twisted off the bottle cap and slowly lifted the bottle toward his mouth. He gulped down a few swallows, set the bottle on the table, and leaned back in the chair. In the dimness, he reached his arms, stretched wide, and then gently laid one arm around Clarisa's shoulder. With a grunt and a sigh, he released his tension.

Clarisa released her hug and looked at him intensely, examining his state of mind. He seemed better now.

Israel proudly sat up. "You had better go, Clarisa. You need to get home to your family."

"I'm not leaving after all of that mess!"

"It's okay, babe, I'm all right. It's you that I'm worried about." Now, much more calmly, he looked into her eyes. "It's okay. I'll walk you home."

"You know I don't need that. I'm just around the corner. Besides, you're hurt."

Clarisa had a suspicion that all of the events of the night were aimed at Israel, not at her.

"I ain't gonna let you go by yourself."

"You don't have to let me do nothin'." She smiled. "You know we all walk where we need to go around here. Besides, I'm not goin' back toward the store anyway."

She knew that Israel didn't want to let her walk by herself, but he knew that once she made up her mind, nobody could change it.

"Okay, go ahead. Just don't go back by those dudes."

"Don't worry. I know how to take care of myself."

Israel kissed her on her cheek. She stood up and felt her way back to the door with her fingers, just as Israel had done. She opened the door, turned around, and blew Israel a kiss. He saw her movements in the shadows, smiled, and blew a kiss back to her. Clarisa could not quite see what he did, but she knew. She smiled, standing there quietly in the dark, watching him sit at the table.

A thin shimmer of light cascaded through the window from the street lamps outside and dimly lit one side of Israel's face. Clarisa could see him now. The face was of a boy, a young teen. He wasn't so young anymore; at least, that's what the streets said. Israel knew how to take care of himself. He had been doing it for quite some time now. Tonight would be no different. He could handle it. He had done it before, many times. Tomorrow, he would see his homeboys and her again. It would be okay. He took another swig from the soda bottle and put it to one side. Slowly, his head lowered and fell into the fold of his arms on the table. Sirens blared outside in the dark. Down the street, a few faint gunshots echoed through the humid night air. He never heard them. He was asleep.

Clarisa decided to leave him where he was. He was rarely at peace. He was at peace right now. She walked out of the door and disappeared into the night of the neighborhood.

A NEW DAY

Loud music blared from Clarisa Sanchez's clock. The sun had not risen yet, but her day, as usual, began when most continued to sleep. Her hand lazily flopped up and hit the top of the clock, silencing the noise. Then it fell like a stone next to her as she rolled over and continued to dream. One side of her mouth donned a slight grin.

In her slumber, she saw herself inside a white marble church. The walls and floors glowed. Ivory statues of saints came to life as their eyes fixated on her every movement. Clarisa stood—no, floated in front of an altar, facing the gathered crowd that sat attentively in rows.

"I...I want to thank everyone so much for coming here today!"

Clarisa now glided down the middle of the aisle and looked into the eyes of everyone in attendance. Her toes pointed down, and her arms stretched out elegantly, as if she were a beautiful ballerina.

"All of you have made me so proud, and I feel so special. You are all the reason that I have made it to this point in my life. Because of your support and love, I float in front of you today!"

Abruptly, one of the benches in the back of the church turned black. Clarisa felt her body lower toward the floor. She focused intently on the black bench that was far away in the corner. She squinted and could see one person sitting there. Clarisa glided down the aisle, closer and closer. Finally, she approached the edge of the bench and hovered in place. A man slid over to the corner and looked up at her. He was a young man with a dark mustache and wore a long, black trench coat.

Clarisa pierced his eyes with hers. "Who…who are you? Why are you here?"

Slowly, the stranger stood. He reached behind his back.

"Sir, what is it? What are you looking for?"

The man continued to struggle with his hidden arms and seemed to fumble and drop something behind him.

"It's okay, sir. You don't need to give me anything. Just you being here is enough."

The man smiled a sad smile as he looked with loving eyes at Clarisa. All of a sudden, his hidden hands stopped moving. Quickly, they reappeared. He was holding in front of her some type of hat.

"What is this? Can I hold it?"

The man released the hat into the air, and it magically glided into her hands. It was beautiful. Ruby red in color, it warmed her heart with love and reassurance. But she could not understand why a hat could do this.

"I … I don't get it. Why is this hat so special?"

The stranger pointed to her head, gesturing her to put it on.

Clarisa placed the beautiful hat on her head. Just then, a mirror appeared and gently floated in front of her. As she looked at herself, the hat slowly changed. Now it was flat on top, and a small tassel hung on one side.

"This … this is what students wear when they graduate. Mister, why are you giving me this? I'm only fourteen years old."

The strange man smiled, but it was a smile accompanied by sadness and hurt.

"Sir, what is wrong? Why are you sad?" She could not take her eyes off of him.

The man, somehow familiar to her now, did not talk. He remained staring at her with the same gloomy eyes. Then suddenly the man began to change. His sadness disappeared, and the darkness surrounding him began to fade away. The black bench turned white again, and the man began to float in the air in front of her. He was almost close enough to touch.

Miraculously, stunning white wings unfolded from his back. A white robe replaced his black coat. He began to rise before her. As Clarisa looked up, the top of the church opened, and radiant blue skies appeared. The man began to ascend faster, and his wings started to flap like an eagle, slowly, with powerful thrusts. As he started to soar upward, he turned around and looked down toward Clarisa. He beamed a warm smile at her.

"Sir, wait! Don't go. I need to talk to you."

The man flew upward into the heavens. As he did so, a radiant rainbow appeared over the church. Gold, glitter-like confetti began to rain down over everyone in attendance. The guests looked up toward the sky as they reached out their hands to catch the raining treasure.

"Sir, don't go! Please, sir. Sir? Papi?"

Just then, the loud music blasted from Clarisa's clock again. This time, the dream stopped.

Clarisa's arm flew out and hit down on the top of the clock once more. She lay there and thought about her dream. She didn't think that it was a bad dream, but it made her feel happy and sad at the same time.

Retreating back under the sheet, she tried to rest just a little bit more before *it* started. When *it* started, everyone had to get up. *It* had been happening every day since the new neighbors had moved in, and *it* was inevitable.

Under the sheets, thoughts abounded.

I guess with my quinceañera coming up, everything is getting mixed up. Even my dreams don't make sense!

Clarisa rubbed her eyes with the palms of her hands.

We all miss Papi. It is hard to remember him. He died when we were so young. But somehow I know he was good. Even though Mamá tells us how great he was, she doesn't have to. I know he was good. I know.

She stretched under the covers. A smirk appeared.

I can't wait until my fifteenth birthday next month! Gosh, it is gonna be great. Finally, I'm going to be a woman. All my primas in Mexico had such nice parties. My friends' fifteen parties in Houston have been wonderful too. I hope Mamá lets me stay out real late on weekends. Man, that would be awesome!

While Clarisa continued to lie under her covers and think about her upcoming quinceañera, the room remained silent. Across the bedroom lay Clarisa's younger sister, Maribel. Although she was one year younger than Clarisa, they had the same birth date. Their mamá blamed this occurrence for the sisters' constant bickering. However, she also told the sisters this was why they were so close to each other.

But we need to get a church reservation soon. What good is my fifteenth birthday without that? I know that we don't have a lot of money, but I should have something. A dance would be awesome! Wow, I can't believe it. I'm almost fifteen—a woman!

In the same room, Juanito, the newest addition to the family, was asleep in his crib. Lying on his stomach, legs bent at the knees and tucked up under his little belly, he looked like a tiny ball. His head was turned to one side with his thumb resting ever so closely to his mouth. Although silent in his slumber, the six-month-old could shake the walls with his cries.

My fifteenth birthday is going to have balloons, music, and food, and all my friends. I'm going to be in a beautiful pink dress, and all the cute boys will line up to dance with me. I'll turn them all down and then pick the cutest one and make him ask me to dance. And then…

And then *it* started.

Boom! Bada bada bada boom! Boom! Boom! Bada, bada, bada, boom! Boom! Boom! Boom!

The tremendous clamor of music blasted from the apartment next door. Every morning, at the same time, the paper-thin walls let the blaring music through. Everything in the bedroom vibrated like a bowl of gelatin.

"Aw, man! Here we go." Clarisa covered her head with her pillow.

The big mirror on top of the old dresser against the wall began to rattle in perfect beat with the music from next door. Perfume bottles on the dresser moved like tiny soldiers in unison before they fell one by one to the floor. Lipstick rolled back and forth. Combs and brushes wiggled with life. Clarisa's body slowly squirmed as she uncovered herself. Like a butterfly escaping from a cocoon, she sat up and rubbed her eyes, knowing that the long day had begun.

Clarisa launched a pillow though the air at her sister, hitting her in the face.

"Wake up, Maribel!"

"Hey! Watch it! You don't have to throw that dumb pillow at me! That stupid music next door makes enough noise to wake up the whole apartment complex."

Juanito's crib began to shake back and forth.

"Here it comes." Maribel sighed, tightening the pillow that her sister had thrown at her.

Juanito's bellows drowned out the neighbor's music. Clarisa arose and walked over to the crib. She gently lifted her crying little brother up from his crib, kissed him on the cheek, and placed his soft, tiny head on her shoulder. His cries stopped. Clarisa smiled. It was a smile full of radiance and beauty.

"Now, now, mi hijito, your hermanita is here to take care of you."

Clarisa stood in the middle of the room, slowly turning left and right, calming her little brother from the rude awakening that they had all just experienced. Juanito cooed like a dove and fell asleep in her arms again.

In many ways, Clarisa was just like a mother to him. She slept in the same room with him. Often, she fed him, bathed him, and even slept with him on her mattress. Maribel loved her little brother too but did not have the same responsibilities.

Maribel reached over from her mattress on the floor and turned on an old, dusty lamp. She squinted at the bright glow.

"Man, I hate this," she complained.

"You hate what?" Clarisa asked.

"I hate getting up this early. This sucks!" Maribel's eyes seemed glued shut.

"Yeah, well, that's too bad."

Maribel rolled over onto her back and put both of her hands over her eyes. "I don't know. I feel kinda sick. Man, I just don't know if I can get up."

"What?"

"My stomach kinda hurts. Yeah, that's it. I've got a stomachache."

Clarisa was wise to her sister's tricks. Maribel sometimes faked being sick so she could stay home from school. Once in a while, Mamá fell for it. Clarisa was having none of it.

"Get up!" Clarisa insisted, kicking the side of the mattress. Maribel's head rolled around like a rag doll.

"All right already! I'm getting up. But it's not gonna be my fault if I get sick all over you."

Clarisa adjusted Juanito from one shoulder to the other. "Don't be gross, Maribel. Just get up, will ya?"

"Okay, okay. And don't forget, tonight I get the bed. You get the mattress on the floor."

"Yeah, yeah, whatever. Move it!"

As Maribel arose and began to show some sign of life, Clarisa remained in the middle of the room, rocking Juanito from side to side in her arms. The small lamp on the floor shed a soft glow. Clarisa gazed around the cramped box they called a bedroom. The only pieces of furniture in the room were a bed, the old dresser, and the baby crib. A mattress, used as another bed, was on the bare wood floor. The floor was good in the summer because when it was hot, they could lie on it and cool down. But the floor was not so good in the winter, freezing their feet with each icy step.

The old, wooden dresser in the corner had been found at the apartment dumpster last year. *Why would anyone throw this away?* Clarisa thought when she lugged it home. The top was cluttered with perfume bottles, makeup, and all sorts of papers, little boxes, and other trinkets. The mirror above the old dresser was half covered with pictures. Some were family. Others were friends.

A few posters decorated the walls. The most special poster was a picture of a beautiful woman. She was the Virgin of Guadalupe, an important symbol of hope for many in Mexico. On a trip to Mexico to visit family a few years earlier, their mamá had bought this poster for them. It showed the painting of a beautiful young woman in a long, multicolored dress, her head covered with a hood that connected to her long robe. Stars twinkled in a half circle above her head. Her face was tan, like theirs, and the Virgin of Guadalupe was staring down toward her feet. Clarisa loved this poster. That's why she put it on the bedroom door, so it would be the last thing that she saw every time she left the room. She liked the thought that someone was watching over her and taking care of her.

Clarisa watched as Maribel stood in the middle of the room. She rubbed her short, poodle-like hair. It was so curly that she almost never needed to brush it. Being about the same size as Clarisa, she often wore Clarisa's clothes if she couldn't find anything of her own that was clean. But the one thing that they couldn't share was shoes. Maribel's feet were too big. They were so enormous that she would sometimes wear Mamá's shoes.

"I'm gonna see if Mamá is home yet," Clarisa told her sister as she walked out of the bedroom with Juanito.

She marched down the narrow hall toward the kitchen, Juanito cooing in her arms. Already, she could smell the wonderful aromas floating down the corridor.

"Mmm. Huevos con frijoles and homemade flour tortillas," Clarisa murmured as she moved closer. Upon entering the kitchen, she saw her mamá putting two plates of food on the small, round kitchen table.

"Buenos diás, mi hija," said Señora Sanchez. "How are you?"

"Hey, Mamá. What's up?"

"Mi hija, what happened last night? Why did you get home so late?" Señora Sanchez moved rapidly from pan to pot.

"Well…I came out of the store with Israel last night. After we crossed the street, some dudes broke into the store and smashed the window!"

"What?" Señora Sanchez walked up to her and caressed her face. "Are you all right, mi hija?"

"Yeah, I'm okay." She started looking at the food that was on the stove. "Israel got hit by a rock. Someone threw it at us. But he's okay."

"Ay, mi hija. This place is so dangerous at night. I shouldn't have let you go last night."

"Aw, Mamá, you know I have to help Israel buy stuff. Otherwise, he gets only candy, soda, and junk food."

"Yes, mi hija, I know. He is a good boy. Just be sure to be careful. And from now on, you two go shopping earlier, before dark."

"Yes, Mamá."

Clarisa always told the truth to Mamá. Besides, everyone knew how it was in the neighborhood. Sometimes, stuff happened.

Now, moving closer to the stove, Clarisa saw many pans and pots with different foods and ingredients in them. Bubbling goodness filled the kitchen with delicious aromas.

Clarisa licked her lips. "What do we have here, Mamá?"

"I have made your favorite breakfast this morning. You go and get Maribel from the room. I don't want your breakfast to get cold. I'll take Juanito."

Their mamá, who cleaned offices at night, was still dressed in her blue work uniform. She arrived at home in the morning just in time to cook breakfast for her daughters, feed the baby, and get ready for her second job at the supermarket down the street. As their mother left the kitchen to attend to Juanito, Clarisa ran back to the bedroom. There, she saw Maribel tossing clothes around the room, apparently searching for something.

"Come on, Maribel, we need to eat fast and get going!"

Maribel was on her knees tossing things out of the closet. "Hey, Clarisa, where are my bunny slippers?"

"How am I supposed to know?"

She searched unsuccessfully. "Did you borrow them?"

"Yeah, right. You have those big dinosaur feet, and you're askin' me if I borrowed your slippers."

"Well, they're not here. Someone had to use them."

Clarisa laughed. "Yeah. I think the neighbors borrowed them yesterday to go fishing. They invited some of their friends and needed a couple of extra boats."

"Will you shut up! You're not helping me here!"

"Why don't you check under the bed where you throw all of your stuff?" Clarisa giggled.

Maribel crouched down and looked under the bed.

"Man!" she exclaimed. "There sure is a lot of junk under here!"

Reaching behind a box, she felt around. Finally, she grabbed a couple of soft, furry things. Pulling them out, she smiled and proclaimed, "Here they are!"

She stumbled from the bedroom, through the hall, and into the kitchen, not quite fully awake. Clarisa closely followed behind her, trying to keep Maribel from bumping into something. They sat down at the kitchen table and each grabbed a tortilla from a covered dish, tore it in half, and filled it with eggs and beans. Breakfast was served!

As the girls ate, curious conversation began, as usual. They always had something interesting to talk about, especially this morning.

"Where were you last night? You got home a little late." Maribel gulped scoopfuls of eggs.

"With Israel, shopping. It was strange."

"What happened?" Pieces of egg hung at the corners of Maribel's mouth.

Clarisa did not show how concerned she had been. "Someone broke into the store after Israel and I left. No big."

"Cool!" Maribel's lips smacked loudly with food. "Hey, you were talking in your sleep this morning."

Clarisa wiped the corners of her mouth with a napkin. "What?"

"Yeah, you were saying stuff like thanks for being here and Papi—weird stuff."

"Oh … well, I had a weird dream about church … my quinceañera I think. Anyway … "

"Yeah!" Maribel gulped down some juice. "You were like, 'I'm so beautiful; thank you; blah blah blah …'"

"Okay, enough. I had a dream about my birthday. It was weird. I think I saw Papi."

Maribel stopped eating. "What! You saw Papi? What … what did he look like? What were you doing?"

"I don't know. I think I was in a church or something, you know, at the beginning of the quinceañera. Anyway, like I said, it was weird."

There was an awkward silence for a few seconds—something that rarely happened between the girls.

"Do you think I'm gonna be in trouble at school?" Maribel blurted as she reached for the salt shaker.

"I don't know. You made Mr. Rodriguez pretty mad yesterday during science class. I mean, what got into you?"

Maribel always did little things in school to get in trouble. Not horrible things, just silly.

"Man, it wasn't my fault. Jose put that green stuff down my back during science lab. I couldn't let him get away with that. Nobody can mess with me like that!"

Clarisa rolled her eyes. "I don't get you sometimes, Maribel."

"What do you mean?"

"I mean, you lose it! You are a ticking bomb that blows up. Why don't you think before you act?"

"You're trying to sound like a grown-up." Maribel continued chewing, scowling at Clarisa.

"Look, Maribel, why did you put that gross pan of earthworms down that guy's pants? Those were part of your science experiment."

Maribel's face beamed with the satisfied look of revenge. "He deserved it!" She chuckled.

"Well, look at all the trouble you might get into. It's not funny."

"Yeah, it is!" Maribel laughed even louder. "And I'll do it again if I have to. That ol' ugly boy makes me sick. He always messes with me!"

"Well, you better tell Mr. Rodriguez you're sorry, and you better hope that he doesn't put you in detention or something."

"Hey, I've been there before. It's no big deal."

True. Maribel had been in the detention room at school quite a bit this year. Not such a nice place. But Mr. Rodriguez was one of the best teachers at the school. His class was the last one that you'd want to get in trouble in. He understood the kids. He got it.

"Look, Mr. Rodriguez has always been very nice with us. You better apologize to him."

"Okay, okay. You're always right and I'm always wrong. I'll go to his room before first period this morning and tell him I'm sorry. Are you happy now?"

Clarisa smiled, knowing that her sister finally had listened to her. "Good."

"Besides, I'm one of his favorite students anyway," Maribel boasted.

Clarisa rolled her eyes and sighed. "You better hope that you are."

After inhaling her breakfast, Maribel scurried down the dark hallway to get ready for school. While Señora Sanchez cared for Juanito, Clarisa, as usual, cleaned the kitchen. It made her happy to help out.

Señora Sanchez prepared Juanito for his daily trip to her sister's house. Because Señora Sanchez had both a night and a day job, their aunt took care of Juanito in the daytime. Tía Maria lived in a small house about a mile down the street from the apartment. Juarez Middle School, where Clarisa and Maribel attended, was on the same street but in the opposite direction. Each morning, before walking toward school, Clarisa and Maribel carried Juanito to Tía Maria's. It was a little out of the way, but this was the only way to give their mother enough time to get ready for her part-time job at the neighborhood supermarket.

As everybody was busy getting ready, Clarisa stood in front of her bathroom mirror and brushed her hair. Silky, dark waves cascaded down her back, stopping near the bottom of her blouse. Sparkling eyes looked dark and magical as she put on her makeup. Her long, curved eyelashes were cat-like. Her brown skin was smooth. All of a sudden, there was a knock at the door.

Clarisa shuffled quickly toward the living room.

"I'll get it!" shouted Maribel, cutting in front of her.

As she rushed to the door, zipping up her jeans, she tripped over a rug in the hallway and hit the floor hard.

"Ouch!" Maribel screamed as she lay across the floor in front of the door.

Clarisa rolled her eyes. "Well, that's what you get. You shouldn't run around like that."

Then the door opened. A young teenage boy stood just outside, laughing hysterically.

"Hey, what's the matter? You guys don't lock the doors anymore?" said Israel.

Maribel pushed her body up from the floor. "Man, what are you laughing at?"

"Uh, maybe I'm wondering why you're on the floor. Does it hurt?"

"I didn't fall! I…uh, I'm…uh, I'm just lookin' for something. And what are you doin' here today anyway?" Maribel asked.

"Why? You don't want me here or what?"

"No, it's okay. I just thought that you wouldn't be here anymore because—"

Israel quickly interrupted her and looked at Clarisa, who was smirking with one hand over her mouth.

"What are you laughin' at?" Israel put both hands on his waist and smiled.

"Nothin.' I gotta go to my room and finish gettin' ready." Clarisa looked into his eyes. "You know, we didn't know you were coming this morning. Mamá doesn't know that you were suspended from school."

"Yeah! You got kicked out of school! Cool!" Maribel gave him a thumbs-up.

"Whatever. Hey, you guys gonna leave me standin' here or what?"

"You want to watch some TV or eat somethin' while you wait?"

"All right, and hey, Maribel?"

"What?"

"Why don't you get up off the floor? My neck is startin' to hurt from lookin' down at you."

Embarrassed, Maribel rose from the floor. "We got some leftover huevos con frijoles in the kitchen. Go get some if you want."

"Tight. Thanks."

Israel headed toward the kitchen.

Clarisa walked into her room and stood in front of the mirror.

This was somewhat of a surprise to Clarisa, but not a bad surprise. Seeing her boyfriend was never a bad thing.

She hadn't thought he was going to walk with them for a while, with the suspension and all. But here he was.

Israel was a good-looking young boy. His short, jet-black hair was always combed toward the back of his neck. He had teeth as white as pearls. Although his oversized black shirt and baggy blue jeans that he wore all of the time made him look malnourished, his presence showed a certain amount of charm and charisma. He always stood up straight, chest out, shoulders back. Proud.

He has had such a hard time but always looks so good.

He spent most of his time at the Sanchez apartment. There were people to talk to there. His older brother was never home at his place. Once in a while, his homeboys would come over. When his mother left two years ago, she said she was going to get a better job and send them money. The money rarely came, and when it did, his brother took it.

Clarisa put on ruby-red lipstick and then gently stroked eye shadow onto her eyelids. Then a cloud of perfume sprayed from a small bottle, almost hiding her in a mist. Before leaving the room, she walked up to the poster of the Virgin of Guadalupe, kissed her fingertips, and gently touched the Virgin on her forehead.

Israel stood over the stove, shoveling tortillas and eggs into his mouth.

"Hey, babe. What's up?" she said, entering the kitchen.

"I'm eaftin' sumf fe stuff yur mufer cookt," he muttered with a full mouth.

"That's okay, you don't have to answer. I'm glad you're here." She slowly walked up to him. Tiptoeing and putting her mouth next to his ear, she whispered, "I didn't think you would be here today. Are you gonna tell Mamá what happened?"

Swallowing his food, he turned to her. "You can tell her. I don't care. I hate that dumb ol' school anyway!"

Startled by Israel's tone of voice, she continued, "I don't know, I just thought, well, you know, with everything that happened in school that you wouldn't be here—"

"Well, I'm here!"

Clarisa looked deep into his shadowy eyes. She could tell that he was upset, even if he didn't say so. "Yeah, you may not care, but you know Mamá isn't going to like it. You know how much she cares about you."

Israel scratched his head, seeming a bit lost for words. "Well, uh, whatever. I don't know. At least you're glad to see me."

"That's right, and don't you forget it!" Clarisa grinned and gave him a light slap on the arm.

Israel grabbed her and turned her around, putting a bear hug around her waist and arms so that she couldn't fight back.

"You can't hit so hard now, can you?" he said jokingly.

"Let me go!" Clarisa laughed out loud. "You think you're a big man, don't you?"

"Big enough to hold you!"

"Well, we'll see about that!"

Israel and Clarisa began to wrestle around the small kitchen, bumping into the table and into the empty dishes on the stove. Loud bangs and thumps could be heard from all ends of the apartment. Maribel ran in.

"Hey, guys, will you cut it out? We gotta get goin.' Mamá's almost ready with Juanito."

Israel and Clarisa stopped play fighting and looked at each other. Israel was breathing heavily. Clarisa was not.

"Looks like you need to do a little more exercising," Maribel told him.

"Yeah, right," replied Israel.

Maribel caught a glimpse of Israel's hand and saw a small cut start to bleed. "Israel, are you okay?"

He quickly closed his hand. "Yeah, I'm okay. Must have cut it on one of these knives here when I fell back."

"Let me see," said Clarisa.

"No … tha … that's okay. It already stopped bleeding," Israel stuttered, hiding his hand behind his back.

Well, I guess it is better than it was last night.

"Okay then. Let's get going. You may not have to worry about being tardy, but we do."

The three of them walked into the living room. This was also Señora Sanchez's bedroom. She slept on the couch after her second job until the kids came home. She was there, changing Juanito's diaper.

"Is he ready, Mamá?" asked Clarisa.

"Un momento," said Señora Sanchez.

She slipped on the diaper and taped both sides firmly. She picked him up, kissed him on his cheek, and handed him over to Clarisa. On the floor next to the couch was a large bag loaded with diapers, baby food, and toys. She handed this to Maribel.

"Man, why do I gotta carry the heavy stuff?"

"Oh, stop complaining, Maribel! Yesterday I handed you Juanito, and you said the same thing!"

"Yeah, well, uh, well … never mind!"

Looking up, Señora Sanchez saw Israel. "Oh, Israel, mi hijo, I did not know that you would be here this morning."

Clarisa shot a mean stare at Maribel. She was the only other person who knew.

"Oops!" said Maribel. "I guess it slipped."

"I'm so glad that you are here to help my Clarisa and Maribel."

"Buenos días, Señora," Israel greeted her. "It's no problem."

"You are such a good boy, Israel. I'm sorry that they won't let you go to school. I heard about the suspension. I'm so very sorry. But you need to obey your teachers. They know what is best for you."

"Yeah, well, they don't like me too much at that school," replied Israel.

"Still, you need your education. That is the most important thing."

"How can I get an education if they won't let me in?"

"Well, you keep your chin up, hijo. I'm sure that when you get back in school, you will show those teachers how hard you can work."

Israel did not answer her. Instead, he grabbed Juanito's bag from Maribel, swung it over his shoulder, and walked outside through the front door, leaving it open. Too busy to give a second thought to Israel's reaction, Señora Sanchez started cleaning the living room. Maribel rolled her eyes at Clarisa, kissed her mamá on the cheek, and headed outside.

"Okay, Mamá, we'll see you tonight," Clarisa said as she leaned over to kiss her mother on the cheek. Señora Sanchez turned around, quickly kissed her and Juanito, and continued cleaning up.

Clarisa hastily exited the front door, leaving it open in her dash from the apartment. As the four of them began their walk toward Tía Maria's house, they could hear Señora Sanchez in the distance calling out, "And remember to learn something in school today so you don't have to work as hard as your mamá when you grow up!"

"We will!" Clarisa yelled back.

It was now six thirty. School started at eight o'clock.

OFF TO SCHOOL

The morning sun glowed a soft burnt orange as it began to lighten the night sky and swallow the stars. Clarisa, with Juanito cuddled in her arms, walked shoulder to shoulder with Israel. Maribel was slightly ahead of them, as usual. Although it was barely morning, the Houston summer heat and humidity smothered them. Makeup dripped in long, black streaks down the sides of the girls' faces.

As the three walked directly east, the rising sun blinded them. Furthermore, there was no sidewalk. The only way was to walk, almost tiptoe, on the edge of the busy avenue. If a car passed too closely, as had happened on a few occasions, there were only two choices: get hit or jump into one of the big ditches that lined the street on both sides.

The streets in Clarisa's neighborhood were infinitely long and flat as pancakes. Walking down any given street was an experience. Next to a home one could find an auto shop or a store, followed by another home and then some other type of business. Graffiti was pasted on the walls of the buildings and homes. Most of it was crude, unrecognizable letters and symbols roughly spray painted on a wall or a fence. However, some taggers (those who painted, or tagged, the walls) were quite talented. Various walls displayed huge murals with beautiful, bright colors and elegant lettering that spelled out a gang's territory and history. Property was helpless to the onslaught of graffiti. Local owners would try to paint over most of it, only to have it tagged again a short time later. So common was the graffiti that most people no longer noticed it. Actually, the surprising part was when someone passed a wall or a fence that was clean. Now that was a sight!

Israel had been walking for a good while with both hands in his pockets, staring at his feet. Finally, he turned to Clarisa.

"Hey, why did Maribel tell your mom I got kicked out of school? Man, I don't like people talkin' about my business."

"I don't know. You know how she is. She's got a big fat mouth."

"I heard that!" Maribel shouted back at her.

Clarisa knew that Israel had been suspended from Juarez Middle School last week because he took a purse from a girl in the hallway between third and fourth period. It was just a joke. He was going to give it back. The girl was actually one of his cousins, but he had been in so much trouble during the past two years that the principal finally decided to suspend him for a whole month. She wondered what he was going to do with all of that extra time. He had always been in a lot of trouble at school, but last Friday was the last straw. However, she was glad that he was here. He usually walked with the girls every morning, first to Tía Maria's house to leave Juanito and then to school.

"Israel," Clarisa continued, "we don't think bad about you, especially Mamá. We know everything will get fixed, somehow."

His nostrils flared as he bit his bottom lip to keep the tears back. "I don't care what anyone thinks about me!"

Surprised by his anger, Clarisa looked at him. "Don't get mad at me. I didn't do anything."

Maribel shot an angry look toward Israel. "Yeah, don't take it out on us. We're not the ones that got kicked out of school!"

Clarisa pointed at Maribel angrily. "Shut up, Maribel! This is none of our business!"

"Whatever!"

Israel just continued to walk silently, looking down toward the ground. Clarisa shifted Juanito to her other arm, reached out, and slowly rubbed Israel on his back. Finally, Israel turned toward her.

"I'm sorry. I just get mad about what happened. The stupid school says I stole a purse! Now, you tell me why I'm gonna steal a purse from my own cousin. Man, I mean, that's my cousin, you know. Me and her are tight like that. We joke around, that's all. This all sucks really bad!"

"Yeah, I know. But you know what the worst part is?"

"What?"

Clarisa smiled. "We won't get to eat lunch together today."

She always could make Israel feel good. Whatever the magic was, it always worked, every time.

"Yeah, you're right. I'll miss ya today." He finally smiled. That smile of his brightened her world.

"Hey," Israel said, "let me hold Juanito. You're letting the sun get in his eyes."

Clarisa waited for a car to race by and carefully handed him over. Israel treated him just as if he were his own little brother. Juanito reached out his arms toward Israel.

One thing that Clarisa admired about Israel was his sense of responsibility toward her and her family. Sure, he had problems. He wasn't perfect. Nobody was. But she could always count on him to watch out for her and her family.

"Here you go, Juanito. Look at this tight chain I got."

Around Israel's neck were a bunch of gold chains. The biggest chain had a medal hanging from it, a big letter *G*. He put this in Juanito's small hand.

"You see, Clarisa, you just gotta know how to chill with the kids."

Smiling, Juanito tried to put the gold letter in his mouth.

"Whoa! Hold on there, little bro." Israel took the little medallion out of his tiny mouth. "You can't have that for breakfast. It took me a long time to earn that letter."

So that's how it was. Clarisa didn't like it much, Israel being a gang member, but then there wasn't much that she could do about it either. Clarisa accepted gangs as a necessary evil in the neighborhood. A lot of the boys she knew were in a gang. Most of them were in Israel's gang. Some girls she was friends with were in gangs too. Several times, Clarisa was asked to join a gang. A couple of times, she almost did. But something inside of her told her that it wasn't right for her to do that. It was okay to be cool with gangs. In some ways, she had to be cool with them. But she didn't want to be a member, and after saying no, they left her alone. Anyway, as long as she didn't cause problems with them, they didn't cause problems with her. She accepted Israel being in a gang because she knew that he didn't have anyone else—no mom, no dad, and most of the time, no brother. What would she do if she didn't have anyone? Anyway, the neighborhood had always had gangs. That's the way it had always been, at least as long as she could remember. The gang in her area was The Gangstas. That's what the letter *G* on Israel's necklace stood for.

As their long walk continued, Israel slowed down and grabbed Clarisa's arm. He raised his eyebrow, paused, and looked into her eyes.

"Hey, Clarisa, why don't you skip school and hang out with me today?"

Clarisa stopped in her tracks. "What?"

"I said why don't we hang out today?"

Clarisa couldn't believe what she was hearing. In the nine months they had been together, Israel had never asked her to do anything like this. Sure, she knew that he skipped sometimes, and now he couldn't even get into the school. But he had always known how important school was to her and had never asked her something like this before. She was a good student. She worked hard. She had dreams. He knew this. Why would he ask her this?

Maribel's steps got faster. "Come on, guys! Keep up!"

Clarisa ignored her and slowed down.

"Israel, I can't. I have a science project due today, and how could you ask me that anyway?"

"Come on, babe. We can go to the park, stay there a while, and then go to the mall. All my homies got stuff happenin'. I don't want to just be bored by myself all day."

Clarisa looked into his eyes. "I can't skip school. Mamá would kill me. And what about Maribel?"

"She don't have to come. It's not like she doesn't know the way to school."

"I…I just can't. You shouldn't be asking me to do stuff like that."

"You just don't love me enough, do you, babe?"

"Israel, you know that's not it."

He handed Juanito back to her and put his hands in his pockets. They both walked silently, staring toward the ground.

The rest of the way they did not say a word. They quickened their pace so that they could catch up with Maribel. Soon they saw Tía Maria's house. It was a small home with a little cement porch in the front that rose about two feet off the ground. Three little wooden steps led up to the front door. The yard wasn't much bigger than the front porch, reaching the street after only a few short steps. The only thing that could fit on the porch was an old, metal chair, and that was almost falling off the side.

Tía Maria was waiting for them.

"Hola, Tía!" Maribel greeted her, panting and out of breath.

"Hi, hijita. How are you this morning?" She walked up to her and kissed her on the cheek.

"I'm fine." Maribel smiled.

She turned to Clarisa. "There's my little Juanito!" Tía Maria always got so excited. As Israel and Clarisa climbed the steps of the front porch, Juanito reached out to Tía Maria. "Oh, my little nephew loves his tía, doesn't he?" Lovingly, Tía Maria took Juanito from her arms.

"Here's the bag with all Juanito's stuff," Israel said.

"Gracias, hijo. Do you three want some breakfast?"

"No, we gotta get going, Tía," said Clarisa.

"Are you sure?"

"We already ate," added Maribel. "We don't wanna be late."

"We'll see you after school," Clarisa said as the three of them left the front yard and walked back to the busy street toward school.

"Adios, niños. Be careful today!"

THE ENCOUNTER

Clarisa, Maribel, and Israel walked back down the same busy street toward Juarez Middle School. It was now seven fifteen. School started in forty-five minutes. They had the walk timed so that they would arrive at the school right about the time the first bell for class rang. But things in this neighborhood didn't always work out as planned.

"So what are you going to do today?" asked Clarisa as several cars zoomed by, blowing her hair over her eyes and face.

"I don't know. Hang out somewhere, I guess." Israel seemed sad.

"Hang out where?" Maribel asked.

"I don't know, maybe down the street with some of my homeboys. Some of them might be hangin' out around the store or the pizza place."

"Who's gonna be there?" Clarisa wanted to know.

"You remember my cousin Abel?"

"Yeah," Maribel added. "I remember that dude. Isn't he the one with the blue low-rider?"

"Yeah, but he totaled that bad boy last month. He's on foot now. Anyway, I might run into him."

Clarisa was a little worried about Israel being on the streets all day, but she figured he would be okay. He knew a lot of people. Somebody always had his back. Usually, the streets were no problem for Israel—usually.

"You gonna walk us home?" asked Clarisa.

"Yeah. I'll be across the street at three."

After a while more, the three finally approached Juarez Middle School. Briefly, they paused in front of a large apartment complex across the street from the school.

The building was two stories tall and extended down the street for at least two city blocks. Weeds that sprouted up in the dirt yard in front of the apartments were the only living plants there. Tan paint that used to be white was peeling off from what seemed to be every board on the sides of the apartment complex. Most of the broken windows looked like dirty, jagged weapons. Despite these conditions, the complex had a waiting list of people wanting to move into them. Rent was cheap, and people were poor.

As they approached the corner intersection across the street from the school, they saw three boys dressed in black and purple standing there, one smoking a cigarette, the other two speaking Spanish and laughing. They all wore purple basketball jerseys that loosely hung like wet

T-shirts on a clothesline. Turning toward them, the three boys shared a devious grin. They were staring at Clarisa.

"Hey, Clarisa, why are those boys staring at us?" Maribel whispered.

"Are they?"

"Yeah, and I think they're staring at you."

Israel turned toward the boys. "Hey, what are you lookin' at, punks?"

The boys slowly strolled toward them in unison, like a slow motion picture.

"Israel," whispered Clarisa, "what is wrong with you? What are you doing?"

"Yeah, what's your problem?" Maribel slapped Israel on the arm. "You want us to get jumped or somethin'?"

Israel stood his ground, staring down the three boys with a hard look.

The three came closer.

Now slightly trembling, Clarisa clutched Israel's arm with a firm grip. Biting her lower lip, she studied the features of the approaching youths. The boy on the left donned a violet stocking cap that made his head look like the top of an ice-cream cone. His dark sunglasses hid the rest of his features except for a thin, shadowlike mustache that protruded out from his upper lip like pricks sticking out of a cactus. A long, dark green tattoo twisted and turned down the skinny arm of the other boy from his shoulder to his wrist. A large gold earring dangled from his left ear, while a jagged, purple scar curved around the top of his right eyebrow all the way down the side of his face, stopping at his chin, oddly making him resemble a stitched rag doll.

"You talkin' to me, you skinny punk?" the boy in the middle challenged, flicking the butt of his cigarette toward the ground, hitting Israel's shoe.

Clarisa's eyes opened wide. *He's got to be the leader. Hey, I think I've seen this guy before.*

"And if I am talkin' to you, what ya gonna do about it, homes?" Israel smirked as he tightened his fists.

As the three boys began to surround them, Israel stared into the leader's eyes. They were black as night. The stranger's pudgy cheeks shaped his face like a donut. Two tree trunks hung from his broad shoulders.

"I might not do nothin'." Number Thirty-Four stepped forward and mumbled close to Israel's face. "Or I might do somethin'."

Maribel and Clarisa moved behind Israel. As the other two thugs circled behind them, the sun's reflection came from the direction of one of the boy's hands, suddenly blinding Clarisa's eyes. Quickly, she glanced away and then turned back, attempting to focus on the boy's palm. It was a blade.

"Israel, he's got a knife!"

STANDING GROUND

Israel was lightning quick. He grabbed a handful of sandy dirt and tossed it in the direction of the tattooed boy's face, splattering it over his eyes and mouth. He flailed his arms, trying to wipe the blinding dust and dirt from his face. In the process, his open palm, holding the knife, was exposed.

"Move!" Israel shouted as he leapt in the direction of the chaos. Clarisa grabbed Maribel's arm, pulling her to one side, bumping into one of the other strange boys in the scuffle. Israel's elbow chopped down onto the tattooed boy's wrist, causing him to drop the blade to the ground. With catlike quickness, Israel kicked the weapon a few feet away onto the curb of the street. As the stunned boy whimpered in pain as he grabbed his forearm, a swift kick to the stomach greeted him, dropping him like a stone.

"Aargh!" the stocking cap boy shouted in pain.

"Israel, watch out!" Clarisa shouted.

At that moment, a leg kicked at Israel's ankles, causing him to fall hard to the ground. Rolling over, Clarisa saw the tattooed boy standing over Israel with an evil grin. As he tried to get up, the boy pinned one of his arms on the ground with his foot.

"Fool, you shouldn't have messed with my homeboy like that," the boy said.

"Get off me!" Israel squirmed on the ground, unable to get up.

Clarisa and Maribel didn't know what to do. To one side, they saw the boy with the stocking cap on his face lying on the ground, still trying to get the dirt out of his eyes. Directly in front of them, Israel was pinned down and in danger. To their left, they saw Number Thirty-Four laughing. The girls' eyes communicated their thoughts. *What is going on? What can we do? How can we stop this whole thing?*

"I said let me up, fool!" Israel shouted.

The boy's foot pressed harder on Israel's wrist. Israel grimaced.

"Why did you mess with my homeboy, fool? Why?" The tattooed boy curled his hand into a ball.

Israel continued to squirm. As he turned to one side, his gold chain with the letter *G* fell out of his shirt and hung over his shoulder. Number Thirty-Four clearly saw the gold letter *G* reflecting in the sun. His grin faded.

"Okay, cut it out. Let the dude up, homes," Number Thirty-Four suddenly stated in a calm voice.

"But did you see what this dude did to our homeboy over there?" The angry face of the tattooed boy turned red.

Now clearly agitated, Number Thirty-Four again demanded, "I said get off the dude! Let him up!"

The boy lifted his foot, and Israel quickly pulled himself to his feet. Clarisa immediately ran toward him.

"What is wrong with you guys?" she began. "What are y'all doing?"

The three boys were standing together again. They didn't answer.

"This isn't right! We were just walkin' to school," she continued.

Stocking cap boy stepped forward. "Your boy there shouldn't have called us out like that."

"Dude, y'all were staring my girl down." Israel stood proud, ready to fight.

"Hey, we can't help it if your girl has got it goin' on. Somethin' is wrong with a man if he don't take a look at what she's got." The tattooed boy grinned deviously.

Israel's eyes flared with anger. Clarisa gripped his arm, keeping him from attacking. "You see! Now you're disrespectin' my girl again! What's wrong with you, fool?"

Number Thirty-Four glared at the guy with the tattoos. He stepped back and was silent. Then the leader turned to Israel. "Hey, man, like my boy said, you called us out, and in our hood. We ain't gonna stand around and let nobody disrespect us like that."

"Dude, your homes right there pulled a blade," Israel answered. "What's up with that? And who said this was your hood, dude? Who are you?"

Ignoring Israel's question, Number Thirty-Four turned around and asked, "Did one of you pull a blade?"

"Yeah, fool," the tattooed one answered.

"Where is it?"

"Over here!" Maribel shouted, walking toward them from the street. She had picked it up from the street and was holding it in her hand.

Everybody stared at her. Nobody spoke. Nobody moved, not even Maribel. Then Clarisa shouted toward her.

"Put it down, Maribel. Now!"

Maribel stared at the blade with awestruck eyes. Raising it up, she slowly turned it in the sunlight, watching shimmering rays reflect off of it in all directions. She was fascinated.

"Fool, what's your homegirl doin'?" Number Thirty-Four shot Israel a nervous look.

He didn't answer.

"I said put it down! Right now, Maribel! Put it down now!" Clarisa shouted.

"All right, all right! I'll throw the stupid thing down. You don't have to yell at me so many times, you know!"

Maribel took the knife and threw it across the street into a large, grassy area. It would be nearly impossible to find it there.

"Fool, she threw my knife away!" The tattooed boy ran toward the street.

"Shut up and stop running," Number Thirty-Four calmly stated.

Immediately, he walked back and stood next to him.

Clarisa now stepped forward, passing Israel and strolling toward the strange group of boys. He put his arm out to stop her, but she walked right through it. "This has to stop." Her voice of calmness seemed to ease the tension.

Clarisa gazed toward the ground at Number Thirty-Four's feet. She raised her head, and her eyes arrived at his. Immediately she cast a tranquil spell on him, almost causing him to smile.

"Please, stop this now. We just want to go to school. Let us go. Please."

Israel stood directly beside her, both fists wrenched tightly.

Number Thirty-Four relaxed his shoulders. Both of his arms fell and hung loose on both sides. The other two boys waited in silence behind him.

Maribel stormed forward like a bull. "Hey, why don't y'all just leave us alone! We didn't do nothin'!"

"Shut up, Maribel! I'm handling this!" Israel told her.

"Well, you haven't handled it so far!"

Clarisa turned. "Maribel, shut up! You're makin' things worse!"

"Don't tell me to shut up! You shut up!"

The three strange boys backed up, watching Israel, Clarisa, and Maribel form a little circle, arguing with each other.

"Maribel, will you just shut up?"

"What are you gonna do, Israel? You gonna beat 'em all up?"

"Why? Are you?" he replied.

"Israel, stop! You know how she gets. You're just gonna get her more mad," Clarisa told him.

"Well, I don't know about y'all, but I'm gonna end this thing now!" Maribel firmly stated.

She pushed her way up toward the three boys. Clarisa tried to grab her shirt but could not hold on to it.

"Y'all think you're bad, don't you?" she said. "You're just gonna beat up anyone that walks by. Well, come on! Beat me up!"

Confused, the three boys looked at each other. They towered over Maribel like skyscrapers, casting dark shadows over her face. With her eyes ablaze, she held up her hands in a boxing position, moving them in a circular motion.

"Stop, Maribel!" Israel and Clarisa both begged.

"Come on!" she challenged. "I'm not scared of you ol' ugly boys!" She continued to move her fists and arms in circles.

Suddenly, the three boys looked at each other and began to laugh uncontrollably.

"Man, this is a trip." The tattooed boy shook his head in disbelief.

"Yeah, a trip," replied the one with the stocking cap.

Even Number Thirty-Four smirked.

"Stop it, Maribel!" Israel finally got a hold of her arm and pulled her back.

"Look," Number Thirty-Four said to Israel, "you and your bodyguard here just watch out where you're walkin' next time. The Latin Posse is movin' into this hood. If you're not down with us, you better watch where you're walkin,' fool."

Israel stood firmly. "Hey, dude, I'm a Gangsta. This is our hood. If you fools want to settle this later, let me know, and my homeboys will be there!"

Clarisa buried her face in her hands, shaking her head in disgust.

Number Thirty-Four smirked like an evil clown. "I guess your homeboys aren't very dependable because you could have used them last night."

Clarisa's eyes widened.

So that was it. Last night in front of the store. That was it. It was them.

She looked at Israel. Israel's eyes were on fire with rage. He had realized it too.

"Like I said, I'm a Gangsta. You dudes can't claim nothin' round here. This is our hood. If you want problems with me, that's okay. You'll have problems with my homeboys too. And as for the girls, you better not even look at them again if you know what's best for you."

The three didn't reply. Just as suddenly as everything had started, they turned around and walked toward the old apartment complex, disappearing into the shadows of a winding stairway and into a dark, dirty hallway, like ghosts.

For a moment, Israel, Clarisa, and Maribel stood there, looking into one another's eyes. The shock of the moment silenced them. After a few seconds, they began to slowly walk back toward the school.

"Hey," Israel said, breaking the silence, "you were pretty brave back there, Maribel. I didn't know you had it in you."

"Yeah, well, you've never made me mad like those stupid punks did back there," she responded.

"They shouldn't mess with you anymore!"

"You were pretty bad back there too! I didn't know you could fight like that. It was so tight the way you kicked that dude!" She smiled at him and gave him a thumbs-up.

Clarisa stopped and turned to both of them.

"That wasn't a game, guys! That was serious, and I don't think you should be talking about all of it like it was a big joke!" Grabbing Israel's hand, she stared into his eyes. "Promise me that you won't go back to those apartments today, Israel. Please, promise me that."

"Man, I ain't gonna walk down no different street just 'cause those fools are over there!"

"Just for me, babe, please! I know you're not scared. Just do it for me. Please."

Maribel smirked. "Aw, here you go gettin' all mushy again."

Israel looked into Clarisa's beautiful, midnight eyes.

"Okay. But just for you. I ain't scared of nobody."

"Oh, thank you. Thank you." She smiled and kissed him on the cheek.

"Man, come on!" Maribel exclaimed, pulling on Clarisa's arm. "We're gonna be late, and I gotta go find Mr. Rodriguez and apologize for that frog stuff I did." Without waiting, Maribel ran across the street, walked quickly down the sidewalk, up the steps, and disappeared through the front doors of the school.

"I better get going too, Israel. Will you meet us here after school?"

"Sure, babe. I'll be right here on the corner."

"Are you okay?"

"Yeah, don't worry. I'm gonna go find Abel down at the store."

"Okay. Gotta go. Bye!" Clarisa blew him a kiss before she ran across the street and into the school.

SCHOOL BEGINS

Students had different opinions about Juarez Middle School. For some, it was a place to learn. For others, it was just a place to be. See friends. Get away from home. Get a free meal. Kids heard teachers talking all the time about them being "at-risk students." They didn't really understand what this meant, but the students knew they were mostly at risk of failing classes or just being plain misunderstood. Juarez wasn't a bad school. It just didn't help all the kids in the way that some of them needed help. Clarisa took school very seriously. She put forth her best foot when it came to learning, and learn she did. She was ranked at the top of her class.

As she walked quickly down the hall toward her locker, the tardy bell rang for first period.

"Dang it! I thought I had more time than that." Clarisa quickly turned the combination to her locker and opened it.

That locker was her home away from home. Pictures lined the inside. Photos of family and friends and cutouts from magazines were taped all over. Clarisa removed her books, slammed the locker shut, and ran toward her first class. The hallway was already empty.

At the end of the hall stood Mr. Rodriguez.

She knew that Mr. Rodriguez looked out for her, and because of this, she worked very hard in his class and was his top student. Although a good teacher to all students, he went out of his way for her. She appreciated that. She always raised her hand and asked good questions. She helped other students. This made his job easier. She liked being in school, and sometimes her enthusiasm caught on with other students. However, at this particular moment, she knew that she was in trouble.

"I'm sorry I'm late, Mr. Rodriguez." She smiled. "I had a problem this morning. You see, I—"

"Clarisa, you know this is the fourth time that you've been late to first period this month."

"Yeah, but you see, I was walking to school, and—"

"You need to make sure that you are not tardy again. I'll be forced to send you to detention next time. That is school policy."

Man … if he only knew what was going on.

She decided to bite the bullet so she could get in class. "Yes, sir. I'm sorry."

Mr. Rodriguez was very strict with his students, but only because he wanted success for all of them. Clarisa knew that he was from the hood, and he looked at all of the kids as if they were family. She knew that because he was from the barrio, he cared about them. He worked hard for them. He was one of them. Just a lot older. He was definitely not your typical teacher, especially at Juarez Middle School.

As she entered class, Mr. Rodriguez had his experiment stations set. The groups already had their goggles over their eyes and their rubber gloves on their hands. Clarisa quickly got her materials on and went to her group.

"Okay, my scientists. Today we are going to study how acids affect different objects. In front of you, you have a small bottle of vinegar and a bag with different objects in them. You—my excellent students—will see what happens to each object as we add vinegar to it."

As Mr. Rodriguez continued to explain and give encouragement, the students began their experiments. One group had a hard time getting started, so Mr. Rodriguez sent Clarisa over to help them. Soon, the group was on their way. After a while, results began to be reported.

"Man, this is cool!" One boy held up a handful of goo. "Look how the vinegar melted this stuff!"

"Yeah, check out this piece of chalk," another added.

Clarisa saw Mr. Rodriguez smiling and helping everyone. How proud he was when the class did their work.

"Yes, yes, Dr. Julio," he said to one boy, "you are correct in stating that the acid is eroding away the outside layer of your chalk."

As the class continued the experiment, time was up before they knew it. They quickly cleaned up, and the bell rang.

Between classes, the hallway turned into an ant colony. Students huddled briefly, exchanging gossip, and then continued on their way to the next class, spreading the same gossip. Kids who thought they were all that slowly strolled down the hall alone, like soldiers, aware of the goings-on around them but silent in their march. Teachers stood at their doorways, the entrances to their caves. Once a student entered their domain, it was the teacher's rules. That's why the halls stayed full until the last thirty seconds, when everyone scattered to their classes at the last moment.

After fifth period, Clarisa approached the restroom on the way to lunch. She didn't really have to go. She just wanted to see what was going on. The restroom was the hot spot during class change. As she walked through the door, a cloud of smoke engulfed her.

"Man, put out the cigarette, girl! My hair is gonna stink somethin' awful!" she announced as she entered.

Bodies crowded together like a herd of cattle in front of the lone mirror on the far wall. Graffiti covered everything, making all who entered feel that they weren't even at school. Conversation and idle chat echoed between the cramped walls.

"Hey, you got some strawberry lip gloss?"

"Who borrowed my hairspray? Hey, give it back!"

"Yeah, I think he's cute, but I wouldn't go around with him or anything."

"I would."

"I thought you did."

"Yeah, I did, but I would do it again if he would text me."

In the corner, a group of girls all looked down into their hands. Their thumbs were speeding across their cell phones with lightning quickness. Cell phones weren't allowed in school, so the bathroom was one of the only safe places to use them.

After pushing her way through a maze of students, Clarisa ran into one of her science classmates.

"What's up, Ana?" Clarisa quickly kissed her on her cheek. Her black eyeliner made her brown eyes look big and beautiful.

"Hi, Clarisa! What's goin' on?"

"Nothin' much, girl. What about you?"

"No luck with a boyfriend this year. I'm still lookin' for a man who deserves a woman like me!"

Clarisa laughed. "Man, you're pretty sure of yourself."

"Hey, how long have you and Israel been goin' around?"

"I guess around nine months."

"Man! That's a long time, even longer than my parents were married."

"It's not that long of a time."

"Well, if you ever break up with him or anything, would you get mad if me and him went together?"

"What!" Clarisa exclaimed.

"Just kiddin,' girl." Ana brushed her hair. "Chill out. I'm not the kind of girl that would go around with a friend's man. That ain't right, you know."

"I ain't mad. I know you're playin.' Hey, can I borrow some lipstick?"

Ana handed it over to her.

"Thanks." Clarisa touched up her lips and smacked them together.

"Keep it, girl. I gotta get goin.' See ya later!" Ana smiled and ran out of the restroom.

It was true, Clarisa and Israel had been together for longer than the normal relationship lasted at Juarez, but it didn't seem like a long time to her. She enjoyed his company. At school, they always sat apart from all the others and ate in a small corner near the snack bar. Israel liked to listen to Clarisa talk about going to college and visiting faraway places. Hawaii. Europe. Indonesia. He didn't really know where most of these places were, but he liked talking to her. He knew that they were far enough away that he would never see them. But because of the suspension, she wouldn't be eating with him nor talking with him about any faraway places today, or any day soon.

I guess I'll see what the girls have been up to. It's been a while since I've eaten with them.

Clarisa had many girlfriends at Juarez but hadn't spent much time with them this year. She and Israel were always together, so she didn't see them too much. Most of them had been together since kindergarten, so they had a close relationship.

Yeah, it will be nice to catch up on some stuff with my homegirls.

"Hey!" someone yelled. "It's lunchtime!"

Clarisa's thought disappeared. The crowd of girls bottlenecked at the restroom door and finally emptied into the hallway.

Clarisa ran up to the front of the lunch line. She quickly got her lunch and looked for her friends. When Clarisa sat down at the table with her homegirls, they were excited.

"Look, the queen has arrived!" one shouted.

"Yeah! Lovergirl is here, and she looks pretty good! Aren't we lucky to have her with us today?" Several girls chuckled as they smiled and gave her a quick kiss on the cheek.

"Okay, okay, that's enough." Clarisa's face glowed pink with embarrassment.

The questions from her homegirls came quickly.

"So what is the deal with Israel?"

"Hey, did the king let you out of the castle today?"

"What happened? We heard that he got kicked out of school. Is he going to get to come back?"

Clarisa swallowed a bite of her pizza and tried to give the girls some answers without telling too much of Israel's business. He didn't like that.

"Well... let's just say that he messed up, but he is coming back. It wasn't that big of a deal what he did."

"Well, we're sorry for what happened. We know he is pretty cool."

"What did he do anyway?"

Clarisa paused. "Like I said, nothin' big. He was just in the wrong place at the wrong time." Clarisa hit a small plastic bag against the table, breaking the top open. She pulled out a small plastic fork and a napkin.

"Well, that ain't right. Hope he gets back soon."

"Yeah, me too." Clarisa took a drink of her soda through a straw. "Anyway, hey, are you guys comin' to my quinceañera? It's comin' up soon!"

Good way to change the subject.

All of her friends became excited as more questions were shouted out.

"Hey, cool!"

"I want to stand in it!" one girl shouted.

"What color is your dress gonna be?"

"I don't know. I like pink, but I like light blue too. What do y'all think?"

"Clarisa, you will look awesome in anything. But I like the pink!"

"Me too! What church are you gonna use?"

"Forget that! What guys are gonna be there?"

Everyone laughed and continued chatting. Clarisa was glad that she got to spend some time with her home-girls. This was a good day. Soon, the bell rang.

The rest of the day went smoothly. The best part of the day was gym class. They played dodgeball. Clarisa got hit pretty hard by the ball in the first game but got a boy back really good in the second game. As he was running back to get a ball, he slipped and fell onto his stomach. Before he had a chance to get up, Clarisa ran up to him and hit him right on his bottom so hard that the ball bounced into the eighth row of the stands, where another class was sitting, watching the action. Everybody was laughing so hard that the coaches had to cancel the rest of class and make everybody go outside and walk around the track until class was over.

Finally, after eighth period, the bell rang. Students filed out of their classes, toward their lockers, and out the front doors.

Clarisa spotted Maribel as she scampered toward her.

"Hey, girl!" Maribel shouted. "I heard about you in gym class. Nice shot!"

"Yeah, that was pretty tight!" Clarisa beamed with pride.

Maribel scratched her curly hair hard with both of her hands. "Let's get out of here; I'm sick of this place!"

As the two started to walk off, Clarisa looked across the street. There was Israel. Then, without warning, someone grabbed Maribel's shoulder from behind.

"Hey! Get your hand off my...oh. Hello, Mr. Rodriguez."

Mr. Rodriguez was always in the front of school at the end of the day to watch the kids as they left.

"Maribel, are you okay?" he asked.

"Yeah, I mean, yes, sir. I'm sorry. I thought it might be someone else."

Turning to Clarisa, Mr. Rodriguez smiled. "So how was school today?"

"It was all right."

"And your mother, how is she doing, with the new baby and all?"

"She's okay too." Clarisa looked nervously across the street at Israel, who was pacing, kicking up dirt and rocks with his feet. "Look, Mr. Rodriguez, I'm sorry, but we gotta go."

He looked across the street and saw Israel. "Oh, I see. So how is Israel doing these days?"

"Okay."

"Yeah, he almost got in a fight this morning," Maribel interrupted.

Clarisa glared at her. "Well, we gotta go, Mr. Rodriguez. Come on, Maribel!" She grabbed Maribel's arm and jerked her up the sidewalk.

Mr. Rodriguez waved good-bye. "Bye, girls. Be careful going home!"

"Way to go, Maribel! Why don't you just get him into more trouble while you're at it!"

"Chill, girl! I didn't mean anything."

The two crossed the street to where Israel was standing.

"What's up?" Israel said.

"Hey, babe." Clarisa kissed him on the cheek.

"Gross!" Maribel shouted.

Israel scratched his cheek and looked down at his feet. "So what did Old Man Rodriguez want?"

Clarisa grabbed his arm and pulled him close. "Nothin.' He just wanted to know how you're doing."

"Did you tell him that it's none of his business?"

"Israel! He just asked me about you. What's wrong with that?"

"I just don't like nobody in my business."

Maribel interrupted. "Well, you're lucky that you have at least one teacher that still likes you."

"Shut up! Who asked you anyway?" Israel's angry eyes flared.

"I asked myself!"

"Hey," Clarisa interrupted. "What's with you two today?"

"Ask him! He's the one that almost got us jumped this morning."

"Hey, look, Maribel, I got some of my homeboys to take care of it. Everything's tight. We won't have no more problems."

"We better not!" Maribel said.

"Let's go and stop talkin' about all this stuff." Clarisa tugged on Israel's arm, and the three walked toward Tía María's house.

"So what is this stuff that you're taking care of?" Clarisa asked Israel.

"Nothin,' babe. Like I said, my homeboys got our back. Don't worry."

Clarisa knew what that meant, so she didn't ask anything else. Usually, when Israel said that something was taken care of, it was. Sometimes it meant talking, and other times it meant fighting. Usually, fighting wasn't necessary. She didn't like that. The Gangstas had so many members that usually nobody would mess with them. However, the fact that Israel belonged to a gang still made her feel uneasy. But what could she do?

Soon, they arrived at Tía Maria's house. They picked up Juanito and were off to the house. That night, Israel stayed for dinner. After dinner, they watched television. By ten o'clock, Israel left.

Maribel raised her arms triumphantly and celebrated her turn to sleep on the bed. Quickly, she jumped onto the double mattress and pulled the sheets up. "Ah…this is the life!"

Clarisa quietly checked on Juanito before lying on the floor mattress and turning out the light. As the moon glowed through the window, illuminating the room with its soft, gentle radiance, Clarisa thought of the events of the day. Looking at the face of the Virgin of Guadalupe on the door, she received comfort from her caring eyes. She began to nod off, and the darkness faded as dreams began.

My birthday party is beautiful! Look at all my friends dancing. I'm so glad that Israel asked me to dance first.

NOT DETENTION!

Boom! Bada bada bada boom!

So the routine started again. Crying. Arguing. Laughing. Eating. Changing the baby. And so on. Israel was on time, as usual. When they got to Tía Maria's house, they decided to stay an extra few minutes to eat some *pan dulce* with milk. After a few polite words, the three left and continued their path toward school. Without Israel realizing it, Clarisa coaxed him down a different side street toward school and away from the apartment complex where the three boys had been yesterday. She said that she wanted to look at a pretty garden at one of the homes there. When they arrived at the front of the school, Maribel rushed across the street, causing a few honks from annoyed drivers. Quickly, she entered the front doors. Clarisa stayed across the street with Israel.

"Thanks for walking us again, Israel." They walked hand in hand.

"Babe, you don't gotta say that."

"I know, but—"

"Hey, you're my girl."

Israel is so sweet sometimes.

Clarisa gave him a big hug. "So where you gonna go today?"

"I'll probably hang out with Abel again. We might chill at his place."

She looked up to him and winked one eye. "Okay, babe. Just be careful."

"You too. And let me know if anyone messes with you."

"Israel, you know nobody ever messes with me at school."

"That's 'cause they know better," he said proudly.

"I gotta go to class. Are you going to be here after school?"

"Yep. Same time. Same place."

"Okay, bye." She kissed him on the cheek. Then she turned around and ran across the street and into the school building.

Just as Clarisa opened her locker, the tardy bell rang for first period.

"Oh, man!" She hit the front of her locker. "That can't be it already!"

She pulled a few things out, slammed it, and bolted down the empty corridor toward science class. Then she saw him at the end of the hall. With pen in hand and pink slip in the other, Mr. Rodriguez was writing before she even got to his door. Clarisa had seen those slips before, but not for her. No, it couldn't be for her. When she reached the door, she began to explain.

"Mr. Rodriguez! Gosh! You see, we were on our way to school this morning, and—"

Mr. Rodriguez looked down as he wrote the discipline slip. "Clarisa, I don't care what your explanation is. I told you yesterday what would happen if you were late to class again."

"Yeah. I mean, yes, sir. I know. But you see—"

"Now, I know this is the first time that you've ever been to the office, and it just might be a good learning experience for you."

"But," Clarisa continued frantically, "you see, there were these three boys yesterday, and, well, they were staring at me. Well, Israel—"

"Clarisa, could you please stop talking for a second?"

"And we went down a different way today because—"

"Clarisa!"

Immediately, her mouth shut.

"I don't care who you were with or where you were going. The fact is that you have five tardies. The rules say that I have to send you to the office for disciplinary measures. You must understand that rules are rules."

Although surprised by his tone of voice, she did understand him and the rules. She knew that he was being fair, that he had warned her before.

But if he would just listen to me.

"Here is your discipline slip. Please report to the office immediately."

Great! Just great!

Clarisa reached her hand up to take the pass from Mr. Rodriguez, slowly turned, and walked down the hall, shoulders slumped and head low.

Clarisa's cheeks glowed pink with embarrassment as she sat in the chair outside the principal's office. She observed the faces of the other students who were in there. The kid directly across from her stared aimlessly at the floor, lightly touching the Band-Aid that covered the bottom lobe of his left ear. Clarisa knew that boys were not allowed to wear earrings at Juarez, but many kept trying. To her, and most of the girls, the Band-Aids looked really dumb. It was better to just leave the earring at home. Directly beside her was a handsome young boy. His dark, wavy hair was perfectly styled. His dimples showed even though he wasn't smiling. However, the big, swollen, bloody lip that he had could not hide the reason he was there.

"Clarisa?" said one of the secretaries as she walked past the row of chairs. "What in the world are you doing sitting back here?"

"Tardies," she whispered shamefully.

"Oh, honey! That's too bad. I just am so surprised to see you here."

Usually, Clarisa was in the office doing favors for teachers during class time. Extra chalk. Markers. A note. A phone call. She was happy to help in any way. Today was a little different.

The secretary disappeared through the principal's door and appeared a few seconds later. "Clarisa, honey, the principal will see you now."

Clarisa quickly entered the office and sat down in a big wooden chair in front of the principal's desk. Slowly looking up, she noticed an aging, pale, large man sitting across from her. His bald head was pink, and his black and gray-peppered mustache was cut unevenly on one side.

Yeah, he's the principal all right.

Without saying a word, she handed him the pink slip.

"So," the principal began, "you are Ms. Clarisa Sanchez. Is that correct?"

"Yes, sir," she politely replied.

"Would you mind explaining to me why Mr. Rodriguez had to send you to the office today? It is a mighty rare occurrence for him to send anyone here."

She paused and thought about telling him the whole story from the past two days. Certainly he would understand. Then her eyes saddened.

Why even try? He's not going to bother with me. Why would he?

"Sir, I've been tardy to his class five times."

His eyebrows rose, forming bushy tents below the wrinkles on his forehead. "Five times! Well, that is quite a streak that you have going, isn't it?"

Clarisa did not reply.

"Also, I don't believe that I have ever met you. You must be one of the good kids."

There was an awkward silence.

"Well, um...Ms. Clarisa Sanchez, I am afraid that five tardies is entirely too many. You need to wake up earlier in order to get to school on time."

Impossible!

"Since this is your first time to the office, I'm going to give you a bit of a break. You are assigned to detention hall for only the rest of today. With good behavior, you should be back in class tomorrow."

Great. Just great.

"Now, young lady, please try to make it on time the rest of the year."

With that last comment, Clarisa was dismissed.

Walking across the hallway toward the detention room made Clarisa's stomach turn cartwheels. "How humiliating … ridiculous," she mumbled to herself. But she could see no way out of the situation. Lightly, she knocked on the door. Nobody answered. Again she knocked, this time a little harder. Slowly, the door opened. First, she saw thick, stubby fingers appear on the inside doorknob through the small door window. Then a large, flabby arm pushed itself forward from the cave. Finally, the humongous, fat body that it was connected to came forth. It— *she*—wore thick, black rimmed glasses that seemed too small for her round, doughnut-like face.

Oh, God, I am being punished a little harshly, don't you think?

"Where is your office slip?" demanded the beastly woman.

Fumbling through her pocket, she located it and thrust the note forward.

"Okay, have a seat in the back of the room. Read the board. Those are the rules. If you break a rule, you get more days. Now go sit down!"

Clarisa didn't like the drill sergeant's attitude, but she held her tongue. As she walked into the room, the stench and heat hit her like a pan to the face. She estimated that more than thirty-five students were stuffed into this room that was suitable for no more than twenty warm bodies. The dingy, tan walls were peeling like a snake shedding its skin. All windows were covered with old, brown pull-down shades, and the graffiti-riddled chairs were in straight rows, occupied by silent, miserable students, some of whom were smirking at her entrance.

This is real punishment. This is prison.

The teacher stood and pointed to a desk in the corner. "Girl, you better get movin'!"

At the back of the room, Clarisa squeezed into the only empty desk left in class. Squinting, she looked at the scribbled mess on the front chalkboard.

> These are the rules of this class:
> No talking.
> Do your work.
> No sleeping.
> Stay in your desk.
> No passes to the restroom.
> Do not raise your hand unless it is an emergency.
> If you break any of these rules, you will be given more days of detention!

Putting her elbows on the desktop and hands over her eyes, Clarisa quietly sighed and whispered to herself, "This is gonna be a long and boring day."

The detention room lady raised an eyebrow. "Excuse me, did you say something young lady?"

Surprised, Clarisa looked up. "Ma'am?"

"I don't know who you think you are, but you can't just come in here and think that you run the place. You've just been given another day! I will inform the principal!"

The rumble of snickering students filled the room.

"What did I do?" Clarisa was dumbfounded.

"Lower your voice! Did you happen to read rule number one?" She pointed at the board.

Clarisa pressed her cheeks with flat hands. "Yes. It says no talking, and I wasn't talking to anybody. I just whispered to myself. That's all."

Annoyed, the detention lady replied, "Well, the rule says no talking. I don't care if it is to someone else or to yourself. Just keep quiet or you will have a third day!" The large lady scribbled on her notepad.

Children chuckled.

"And that goes for the rest of you too!"

Nearly in tears, Clarisa looked down at her desk. She wanted to walk up to the oversized windbag and punch her in the nose. She figured that Maribel would try a bad idea like that. Taking several slow, deep breaths, she closed her eyes, calming herself.

This can't be happening. How will I make it in here two days?

Rule copying seemed to be the thing to do. She had no work and was afraid to just sit there and risk getting in trouble again. She picked up her pencil and began. At the beginning, her printed letters were immaculate. Every *t* was crossed, and every *i* was dotted. After thirty minutes, Clarisa was biting her tongue, but her beautiful script continued to have its lovely, looping flow. After an hour, her hand began cramping. After two hours, the lovely handwriting became scribble. Five minutes later, everything coming from the pencil was unreadable.

I can't take this much longer!

Clarisa slowly rubbed her aching eyes and massaged her cramped writing hand. Then she had an urge.

Uh-oh. I gotta go.

Raising her hand got her no attention, not even from any of her co-prisoners. Most of them were busy copying away. Finally, seeing no other alternative, Clarisa stood and approached the large lady's desk.

"Ma'am, may I go to the restroom?" She crossed her legs at her ankles.

"We all go to the restroom at eleven thirty. You'll have to wait. Go sit back down."

"But Miss, I gotta go really bad," Clarisa whispered, embarrassed that someone might hear her.

"I said that we all go to the restroom at eleven thirty! Now sit down!"

Snickers and evil grins came from the seated students. Humiliated, Clarisa went back to her seat. She crossed her legs and bit her lower lip.

With eyes closed, she imagined that she was in a hot desert with nothing but sand around for miles. However, the desert soon turned into a tropical rainforest with waterfalls on all sides. She couldn't hold out for much longer.

The hands of time moved slowly. Beads of sweat began to form on Clarisa's forehead, and her legs began tightening up because of the constant squeezing. Finally, the woman stood.

"Okay, children, line up at the door. Girls on the left! Boys on the right! No talking!"

Thank you!

Upon returning from the restroom break, Clarisa noticed that there were brown paper bags sitting on top of everyone's desks. Sitting down, she just stared, afraid to do anything without the detention lady's permission.

"Students," she began, "you have fifteen minutes to quietly eat your lunch. Make sure that you put all of your trash inside the bag when you are finished."

Clarisa picked the bag up and opened it. She reached inside and pulled out something that looked like a piece of rubber between two pieces of cardboard.

Gross!

Suddenly, she felt a hand tap her on the shoulder. It was the boy sitting beside her.

"Hey," he whispered, "I know this stuff is pretty bad, so do you want a candy bar or something? I brought an extra today."

How nice of him.

But before Clarisa had a chance to answer him, the detention lady shouted from the front of the room.

"Did I tell you to talk? I didn't tell you to talk! Nobody told you to talk! I know he can't tell you to talk! So why are you talking?"

Trying to make sense of the rapid fire of words, Clarisa could only get the nerve to say, "He just wanted to know if I wanted something to eat."

"I doubt that," she continued. "I'm giving both of you another day of detention. Y'all need to follow the rules, students!"

Mean laughter erupted from the others.

"Aw, Miss!" the boy cried out.

"That's right, and you two had better not have another conversation!"

With that, it was all over. And for Clarisa, she thought that the nightmare would never end.

The rest of the day was spent in perfect boredom and monotony, copying rules and waiting, waiting, waiting for the bell to ring. Clarisa had no idea how she would make it with more days in detention added to her original days. She didn't want to think about it.

I don't get it. How did Israel and Maribel even make it through one day? This place is awful. No wonder Israel doesn't look too depressed being suspended. At least he isn't in here.

Finally, after what seemed to be years, afternoon announcements came on. Following a few unintelligible comments, the school bell rang, and the prison doors opened. Clarisa didn't even think about her locker. Instead, she headed straight toward the front of the school. She jogged down the front steps and stopped at the bottom. Slowly, she gazed up at the blue sky, letting the sun warm her face. She slid her fingers through her hair, exhaling hard, releasing the stress of the day. Then everything went black. She felt two hands come from behind her, pressing over her eyes.

"Hey!"

Whoever it was kept holding on tight.

"I know it's you, Maribel."

The hands came off, and Clarisa turned around.

"Hey, what happened to you today? I didn't see you the rest of the day."

"I got put in detention."

She laughed uncontrollably. "What? You?"

"Shut up! Stop laughing at me!"

"I never thought Little Miss Perfect would ever get in so much trouble!"

Clarisa wanted to pull her sister's hair out.

Maribel continued, "I mean, nobody cares when I go to detention. But you? I can't believe it!"

For some reason, Clarisa wasn't mad anymore. Her eyes clouded up. Then the tears began to fall. Maribel stopped laughing.

"Clarisa! What is it? I mean, come on. I'm just messin' with ya."

Roughly wiping the tears away from her eyes, Clarisa said, embarrassed, "I just…I don't know. I don't know why I got in so much trouble. I mean, I know why, but I don't really feel like I did anything wrong."

"Hey, girl, this ain't nothin' but a thing. It ain't no big deal. I've been in there lots of times. All you gotta do is not talk and copy the stupid rules."

Clarisa swept the rolling tears away from her eyes and off her cheeks.

"You know what?" Maribel continued. "I'm gonna find that big ol' lady and ask her what her problem is!" She stormed back toward the school doors.

Surprised, Clarisa ran toward her and grabbed her arm. "Stop! Don't do that!"

"Hey, I'll take care of that big, ugly, four-eyed, wig-wearin,' bad breath smellin,' raggedy clothes wearin' cow for you!"

And with those words, the sisters looked at each other and began to laugh hysterically.

"Man, you sound like you know that lady really well." Clarisa wiped happy tears from her eyes.

"Hey, you get put in there seven times and tell me you don't know her good." Maribel bent over to catch her breath.

A good laugh was just what Clarisa needed. As the sisters turned and walked toward the street, Clarisa began to contemplate her situation.

"I don't know, Maribel. Two more days. I don't know if I can do it."

"You can do it. Just take care of business."

Israel stood across the street, waving at them. After running across the busy street and avoiding a few speeding cars, they arrived at his side. But there was something wrong. One of his eyes was dark black. As he raised his hand to hide it, Clarisa noticed his purple, swollen knuckles.

"Israel, what happened?" Clarisa gasped.

"Nothin,' babe. I ... I fell down on the way over here."

"Yeah, right." Maribel didn't believe a word of it.

Clarisa reached out to him. "Israel, tell me what happened!"

He looked away from the girls toward the ground.

"Tell us!"

"Okay! I'll tell you. Me and my homeboys had it out with those three punks from yesterday."

"What?"

"That's right. They won't be messin' with us anymore."

Clarisa was very surprised. Sure, she'd seen Israel fight before, but strangely, that wasn't what she was so upset about. He had told her that he wasn't going to do anything. He had lied to her.

"Israel, why did you do it?" She touched his cheek.

"What do you mean, why did I do it? They're a bunch of punks, and they were disrespectin' me … you too. You know I gotta save face. I had to do it."

"You lied to me, Israel! You promised me that you wouldn't fight!"

"No, I told you that I wouldn't go near those trashy apartments, and I didn't!"

"Then what happened?"

Israel explained to them how he was down at the store with Abel when the three boys came walking by. "They started flashing their gang signs at us, so Abel got on his cell and got a few more dudes to meet us at the store. They wouldn't even leave after my homies got there, so there was nothing else to do but make them leave. The Gangstas outnumbered them, so the fight didn't take long. I was the first one to jump in, so I got hit a couple of times. Then the three of 'em got jumped by my homeboys. That's what happened, and it's no lie."

"Man, that's bad!" said Maribel. "You mean you jumped all three of them?"

"Yeah," Israel answered proudly.

"That's tight!"

Clarisa put her hands on Israel's cheeks. "Still, I don't know why you had to fight, Israel."

"Come on, babe! You know how it is. I had to do it."

Maribel snapped her fingers. "Yeah, Clarisa, you can't expect them to just let those three do whatever they want."

For some strange reason, Clarisa knew that Maribel and Israel were right. She had lived in the area long enough to know how it was. Respect sometimes had to be earned, even if it was by fighting and getting your homeboys to back you up. That didn't mean she had to like it, especially when it involved Israel. But reluctantly, she accepted it. Still, it didn't feel right.

"Come on, babe. You know I don't fight all the time, just when I have to." Israel pounded his fist into his hand.

"Whatever, let's just go. I wanna get out of here."

"Yeah, she got detention today and has it for two more days!" Maribel smirked with delight.

"What?" Israel gasped.

Clarisa held his arm and pulled it tight. "Yeah, I'll tell you about it later. Let's just get goin'."

On their way, cars flew past them, seemingly closer than usual. Maribel, more than once, had to yell at them after almost being knocked into a ditch. Minutes seemed like hours. Sweat dripped and makeup flowed. When they finally arrived at Tía Maria's house, she was waiting for them on the porch. Israel waited around the corner while the girls went to get Juanito. His cries seemed louder than usual. During the walk home, Maribel shouted at a few more cars that swished by. Clarisa and Israel took turns carrying Juanito. His erupting cries that lasted all the way home almost put the three over the edge.

After arriving at the apartment, Israel decided to go home, avoiding Señora Sanchez's remarks about his face. Trying to enter without waking their mother, the girls went to their room. However, Juanito's bellows woke her. She went to the room, took the crying child from them, headed toward the bathroom, and gave him a soothing bath. The sisters went around the apartment opening windows and turning on fans. The heat inside was almost unbearable. After opening the last of the windows, the girls collapsed on the wood floor of their bedroom.

"This was a really, really bad day!" Clarisa boldly stated.

Maribel reached her arms and legs across the floor. "Yep."

"I've never had a day like this."

"Yep."

"I hate that detention lady!"

"Yep."

"Do you think I should tell Mamá about what happened?"

"Nope."

"But what if she finds out?"

"You're gonna get in trouble either way. Better later than right now. I still want her to make dinner for me."

"Hey, thanks for caring so much," Clarisa barked.

"Any time." Maribel smiled.

After a few moments, the sisters fell asleep and took a short nap. When they awoke, they could smell onions, green peppers, and fajitas. Clarisa and Maribel staggered like zombies into the kitchen. Clarisa uncharacteristically shoveled food into her mouth, not having eaten all day.

Mamá and Juanito joined the sisters for dinner. Afterward, Señora Sanchez quickly ran to get ready for work. Maribel took Juanito into the living room to play and watch TV. Clarisa went straight to her room after cleaning up. Lying down, she gazed around the room.

What am I going to do tomorrow?

Looking at the door, she saw the Virgin of Guadalupe poster.

Where were you today? A lot of good you did watching over me.

CLARISA'S CHOICE

Music blasted from the clock as Clarisa's hand hit hard on the snooze button, knocking it to the floor, waking Maribel and shocking Juanito into loud cries. Señora Sanchez ran into the room.

"What in the world is going on in here?" their mamá demanded as she picked up Juanito from his crib.

Maribel pointed at Clarisa from under her sheet. "Clarisa knocked the stupid clock down!"

"Hijita, what is wrong with you?" asked Señora Sanchez as she uncovered Clarisa with her free arm.

"I don't feel good, Mamá." She squeezed her pillow on top of her face.

I really don't want to go to that dumb detention room today. It will be horrible.

"Ay, hijita, let's see what's wrong with you." She touched Clarisa's forehead with the back of her hand. "You don't really feel too hot, you know."

"Don't let her get away with it, Mamá," said Maribel. "You always make me get up!"

"Are you really sick, hijita?" asked Señora Sanchez.

"Well…" Clarisa began.

Maribel pointed her finger to the ceiling. "No! No, she isn't!"

Clarisa ignored her sister's accusations.

"Now, Maribel, if your sister is really sick, you should not be making such remarks to her." Looking down at Clarisa, she continued, "Let me call into work and tell them that I have to stay home with you today."

Now, feeling guilty that her mother might have to miss work just because she did not want to go to detention at Juarez, Clarisa sat up. "Well, Mamá, let me eat something and see if I feel better."

Señora Sanchez smiled. "Come, hijita, Juanito and I will make you some special tea with your breakfast!"

Mamá and Juanito left for the kitchen.

"Ha!" Maribel put both hands on her hips. "You have to drink that gross tea that tastes like medicine! Good! It serves you right for trying to skip school. You just don't want to go to detention."

"Shh! Mamá will hear you!" Clarisa whispered.

"Look, I'm sorry you have to go, but hey, those are the breaks! You can do it!"

Maribel is right. I should just get up and get going. Sitting in that room all day is going to be awful. Choking down Mamá's special tea isn't going to be much better.

After a few moments, Clarisa arose from the bed and walked into the kitchen. Juanito was in his high chair painting his face with the eggs their mamá had made him for breakfast. Señora Sanchez hovered over a big, blue pot at the stove. Inside the pot was an assortment of sticks and leaves, used to make the special brew. After Clarisa sat and ate a small plate of eggs beside her little brother, Señora Sanchez set a large, steaming cup of tea in front of her on the table.

I guess I better drink this gunk, or Mamá will know something is up.

Maribel walked in, saw the cup, and smiled from ear to ear. She was enjoying seeing Clarisa squirm. Trying not to taste the gooey stuff, Clarisa held her nose shut with two fingers, tilted her head up, and gulped the concoction down. A horrible frown appeared on her face.

"Mmm, nothing like the taste of warm, sour poison in the morning!" Maribel put her fingers in her mouth and gagged.

"Shut up, Maribel!" Clarisa snapped.

After breakfast, the morning went as usual. When Israel arrived at the apartment, he waited outside again so that Señora Sanchez would not see his face. They dropped Juanito off at Tía Maria's house and began the walk back to school. The purple spot on Israel's cheek was not swollen anymore, and his eye was more gray than black. This time, it was Clarisa's head looking down, dreading her entrance to school. How was she going to make it in there those extra days? How embarrassing.

"Babe," Israel started, "it's gonna be okay. Like your sis said, just do your time and get out of there. I've been with that fat windbag more than anyone. Just chill. You'll make it."

"I … I just don't feel like going to school and sitting in detention hall all day!" she complained.

"Just don't go."

Israel's words played over and over in her head.

Just don't go …

Clarisa squinted her eyes as a strange, perplexed look engulfed her features.

What's the use of going to school today? I'm gonna sit all day in a hot, smelly classroom. I'm not gonna eat. I'm not gonna be able to study or talk. I'm not gonna see any of my friends. I'm not gonna see Israel. I'm just gonna sit there all day like a brainless zombie.

Maribel was walking ahead of them as usual. Approaching the apartments where they had had problems two days before, all noticed that there was nobody there today. It was safe.

It's gonna be a really boring day. I'm not gonna learn anything. It's a big waste of my time. Why should I go? I shouldn't. Maybe I won't go. Why not?

Maribel was the first one to make it across the busy street to Juarez's front doors. Clarisa saw her stop at the school doors and turn around to look at her.

Go in, Maribel; go in.

Maribel motioned for Clarisa to cross. She did not move. Maribel looked confused.

Go, Maribel.

Then, in the distance, Clarisa saw Mr. Rodriguez walk outside and stand next to Maribel, talking to her. Maribel shrugged her shoulders and pointed toward Clarisa and Israel. Mr. Rodriguez looked up at them. Her heart pounded.

She grabbed Israel by the hand. Clarisa felt a rush of excitement. Looking into his eyes, she blurted out, "Hey, I'm gonna stay with you today!"

A speechless expression overcame Israel. "What?"

"I'm not going to school to be in detention all day. I want to be with you."

Israel could not find any words to say. "Babe, are you sure you want to do this?"

Now, with a new feeling of exhilaration, she replied, "Yeah, sure! Let's just do it! There's no way I'm going to stay in that stinky room all day."

"But Clarisa, are you sure that—"

She put her hands on both sides of his face. "Listen, do you want to be with me or not?"

"Yeah, sure, but—"

"Then this is our chance! I know what I'm doin'. I'm not a baby, you know."

Now Israel only needed a second to be sure about his reply. "All right then, come on!"

They both looked across the street. Maribel and Mr. Rodriguez stood there looking at them.

Israel grabbed Clarisa's hand and scampered down the sidewalk with her.

"Where are we going, Israel?"

"Let's go down to the store so I can talk to Abel. After that, we can decide what we're gonna do."

While jogging down the street hand in hand, Clarisa turned and could see Juarez Middle School disappearing in the distance. As the two slowed their pace, her heart stopped racing, and her breathing slowed.

I can't believe I'm doing this, but anything is better than staying with that ugly, fat lady in detention all day!

They walked. A strange silence surrounded them.

I wonder what Maribel and Mr. Rodriguez are thinking. Does he know I'm not goin' back? Nah, he's too busy, and Maribel would never think about it anyway. She's too scatterbrained. I'm not goin' back. Well, what can happen in one day? I'll be back after school, and we can all walk back together. It'll be all right.

Soon, they approached the old, graffiti-tattooed store where Abel hung out. Rotted trash littered the broken pavement in the small front parking lot. Filthy, raggedly dressed old men sat on the curb next to the entrance. They passed a bottle wrapped in brown paper between them, each taking quick gulps. Next to the men were a couple of benches. Israel saw Abel sitting and talking on his cell. Quickly, they ran to him.

Israel punched Abel on the shoulder. "What's up, fool?"

Abel held up his hand, signaling him to wait until he finished talking to whoever was on the cell with him. After a few seconds, he closed the phone and turned to them.

"What's up, cuz?" He and Israel exchanged a long, special handshake that the Gangstas had. Then he turned to Clarisa. "And you, little woman? What's up?"

Clarisa stared at his hand. She had learned the handshake before but wasn't sure if she quite remembered it.

She gave it a try. Her fingers twisted up, then down, and then around his wrist.

"Not bad, little one," Abel continued. "You almost got it."

"So what's up for today?" Israel rubbed his hands together.

Abel lit a cigarette. "Nothing yet, just waiting for a few calls."

"I guess those punks won't be showing up around here today." Israel laughed.

"Not after the way we kicked their tails yesterday. They won't be back for a while."

Clarisa turned away. She didn't care much for all the macho talk about fighting.

"So," Abel continued, "what's the little woman doin' with ya?"

"She decided to chill with me today."

Abel slowly looked at Clarisa from head to toe. "Man, you got yourself a good little girl there."

Clarisa remembered why Abel wasn't one of her favorite people.

"So, Israel, what are you guys gonna do?" A cloud of smoke surrounded Abel's face.

"I don't know. We might take the bus to the mall. You got any cash on ya?" Israel tapped his empty pockets.

"Don't sweat it, cuz. I got ya covered." Reaching into his pocket, Abel pulled out a roll of bills. He handed Israel a fifty and some change.

"Fool, this is too much," Israel said.

"Hey, you're my bro. Don't worry about it. I got your back."

He shoved the money into his pocket. "Thanks, dude."

"Hey, Israel, when you get back from the mall, swing by my place. We can all chill there for a while."

"Okay. Later, and thanks for the cash."

"Yeah…later." Abel walked to the back of the store and turned around the corner.

Israel turned to Clarisa, grabbed her hand, and began walking to the bus stop. "Do you want to go to the mall, Clarisa?"

"I…I'm not sure," she said reluctantly.

"What do ya mean you're not sure?"

Clarisa nervously twitched her lip. "I mean, we could get in trouble."

"With who?" Israel protested.

I guess all the teachers are at school. The mall is as good as any place to go to.

Clarisa shrugged her shoulders. "Okay, I don't care. The mall sounds good to me."

The two of them walked to the bus stop in front of the dirty convenience store and waited. When the bus arrived, they got on.

They sat in the back of the bus. The massive engine roared as it puffed out big clouds of black smoke from its tailpipe into the morning air. Like the buildings in the neighborhood, the outside of the bus was riddled with graffiti. Inside was a mass of people heading to work. Speeding down the busy street, the bus hit pothole after pothole, jerking people back and forth like rag dolls. Clarisa and Israel sat in their seat, rocking back and forth in unison with the crowd. One old woman caught Israel's eye, barely able to hold herself up with her bent, frail legs. Standing up, he offered the woman his seat next to Clarisa. Relieved, she sat down.

"Why, thank you, young man." She put her purse on her lap.

"No problem," he replied.

The elderly, gray-haired woman looked over to Israel and then at Clarisa with a curious eye. "My, you two are awfully young. Shouldn't y'all be in school about now?"

Nervous by the question, Clarisa stuttered, "We…uh…we're…uh…we have to…uh…"

"We're…going to see the doctor." Israel stood tall with his back straight.

"The doctor?" said the old woman skeptically.

"Yeah, I'm her brother. I'm taking her there."

She raised an eyebrow. "Uh-huh. And how did you get out of school?"

Pausing, Israel thought of a good lie. "I decided to get a physical. I'm playing basketball this year, and the coaches said that I need to get a physical."

Clarisa lowered her head and covered her eyes with one hand.

The woman stared at them. "Uh-huh…so what's wrong with you, dear?"

Raising her head, Clarisa joined Israel in the game. "Well, uh, my stomach has been hurting for some time now, and it hasn't stopped. So my mom told me to go to the doctor."

"Where is she?"

Clarisa smiled with gritted teeth. "At work."

"Uh-huh." The old lady sat there silently staring out of the window.

Clarisa looked down again. She was not a good liar and was afraid that the old woman might figure them out. Israel remained standing, apparently not bothered by the conversation.

"Well, you probably don't need to be going to the doctor for something as simple as an upset stomach. I make a tea that can cure almost anything that makes a person feel sick," the elderly woman stated proudly.

That must be every old person's cure for sickness. Gross tea.

Israel looked stone-faced at her. "Well, I'm taking her to the doctor."

"I know…you just told me that a few seconds ago." The woman scratched her hand.

The three of them didn't speak for the next few minutes, rocking back and forth, up and down, as the bus roared on its way.

Does this lady know something? Is she gonna tell someone about us?

"So what school do you two attend?" she began again.

"Juarez Middle." Israel smiled politely.

"Juarez, huh? That means you two are in the seventh and eighth grades."

Clarisa jumped in. "We're both in eighth grade."

"Both of you are in eighth grade?" The old woman rubbed her chin. "How can that be? I thought you were brother and sister."

Uh-oh!

"We're…we're twins." He looked at Clarisa and put his finger over his lip, signaling her to be quiet.

"Twins? You two don't look anything alike. How can you be twins?"

Yeah, Israel. How can we be twins?

"Well," he began, "we're … uh … we're … uh … we're that kind of twins that don't look alike."

"Uh-huh." The old lady smacked her lips.

Clarisa wasn't sure how the conversation was going and whether or not the old lady was buying any of it.

Suddenly, the bus made one of its many quick, jerky stops. The old woman got up, thanked Israel for letting her sit down, and exited the bus. Clarisa sighed in relief.

"Twins? You and I are twins? Give me a break!" Clarisa shook her head.

Israel shrugged his shoulders. "Hey, it's the best I could come up with at the time."

Clarisa and Israel had a good laugh as the big bus continued its smoky, bouncy route toward the mall. School was the last thing on their minds.

When the bus finally arrived at the mall, Clarisa and Israel jumped off and walked through the parking lot. Only a few lone cars spotted the parking spaces. They walked up to the huge, locked doors at the front of the mall and sat down on a bench under a tree.

Clarisa looked at Israel. "Hey, babe, have you come here before in the morning?"

He held her hand. "Yeah, I've been here a couple of times when I skip. But it's too far away to come too much."

She caressed his hair. "You don't feel a little weird?"

"Weird? Are you kiddin'? I'm here with the only girl I care about in the world."

Clarisa beamed. "You are so sweet."

They sat silently for a bit, and in the silence, Clarisa began to think.

"Israel, why do you stay with me? I mean, don't you think I'm boring?"

Surprised, he turned to her. "What? What do you mean? Why would you say somethin' like that?"

"I don't know." She let his hand go and stood up. "I mean, you can get any girl you want. Your homeboys don't like me too much. I know it."

"Man, it don't matter what they think." Israel now stood next to her. "What goes on between me and them is my business. We all respect each other. They respect me. We all do what we want, but we are there for each other when we need to be."

Clarisa turned to him and looked into his dark eyes. "I know, but…why me? Y'all don't think I'm a nerd or somethin'?"

Israel chuckled. "A nerd? Man, you ain't no nerd. You…you are just smart, that's all. Ain't nothin' wrong with that. Just smart. Wish I had your brains."

She grabbed his hand again. "But you're smart too, Israel."

"Nah, I ain't smart. I mean, I can do stuff if I gotta do it, but books and school ain't for me." He looked with pride at her. "I do what I gotta do. But you…you got it all…and you got dreams too." Israel seemed to gather energy from Clarisa's hand. "You got what it takes. It don't matter what anyone thinks. I'm with you 'cause you are my girl."

Clarisa was so glad to be with Israel today. They waited outside the mall until it finally opened.

When they walked in, all of the stores in the mall were still closed. The shoe store had a big, metal gate standing in front of it. The clothes store had a thick, glass wall over the entrance. All of the other stores were locked up too. As they looked down the long, empty mall, they saw it was completely vacant. Clarisa listened to the loud clip-clop of her shoes as they echoed down the large corridor.

"This is weird," she mumbled.

"Hey," Israel said, "just imagine if they opened the mall only for us and they said that we had ten minutes to take whatever we wanted—"

"Yeah, you wish." She slapped him on his arm.

"No, really, think about it. Let's say you had ten minutes to take whatever you wanted. What would you take?"

She stared at him. "Well, you tell me. What would you take, Israel?"

"Me? Man, that's easy. I'd go to that shoe store over there and take me all the new basketball shoes." He pointed at the shoe display in the window.

"Why? What are you gonna do with all those shoes? You can only wear one pair at a time, you know."

Smiling, he said, "I'd give the rest of them to my homies."

Clarisa squinted at him. "Then what? You'd still have so many left over."

He thought for a moment. "I guess I'd sell the rest of them or somethin'. Man, those shoes cost over a hundred dollars a pair. I could get some good cash. What about you? What would you do?"

Clarisa thought. Then she smiled.

"I would get some new beds."

Israel looked confused. "What? Beds?"

"I'd get some new beds for Mamá, Maribel, Juanito, and me. Big beds. Beds where you can lay all over the place and still have extra room. Maybe I'd get some big blankets too!"

"Beds? That's dumb. How would you carry them out? You only have ten minutes." Israel shook his head.

"It's not dumb! Besides, you didn't say that I had to find a way to take anything. You just asked what would I take." Clarisa stepped more quickly.

Israel laughed. "Man, you could have thought of somethin' better than beds, like a new MP3 player or some clothes."

Now he was getting her mad. She didn't like being told that what she wanted was dumb.

"Look, that's what I would do! If you don't like it, then tough! It's better than being stuck with a bunch of stupid shoes that don't fit!" She stomped her foot on the ground.

Israel put both hands up. "Okay, okay, chill out! You can get whatever you want in fantasy land. I just wish I had some real cash."

"I thought Abel gave you some money."

"Oh yeah!" He reached deep into his pocket and pulled out the bill. "I forgot 'cause I ain't never got no money. So where ya wanna to go?"

"I don't know. Let's go check out Mr. Music. There's a new CD I want to look at. Then we can eat."

"All right. Let's go."

Gates began to rise, and glass walls began to slide open. Slowly, people began to dot the wide corridors of the mall, all marching to the tune of their own lives, unaware of one anothers' histories.

While in the music store, Israel went to the other side to look at some posters. At a counter, Clarisa busily flipped through some of her favorite music.

Man, I'm in deep now.

Briefly, she thought about how this was the first time she had ever skipped.

Oh well, I'll deal with it later.

She pulled out a CD of a Spanish music artist that sang her favorite love songs. Looking on the back of the CD case, she read a few of the lyrics to a song that she loved.

> *No time to stay,*
> *No time to wait,*
> *Don't stay where you are,*
> *If it's something you hate.*
> *The future is yours; it is in your hands.*
> *Move to the stars, while giving others all you can.*

Clarisa pressed her finger to her head and thought about these words. What did they mean to her? She wasn't quite sure, but in a way, she felt as if the song was written only for her. The lyrics reminded her of her home, the barrio, and school.

School? Oh, man, I wonder if anyone has missed me today. I wonder if Mr. Rodriguez and Maribel miss me.

Clarisa frowned. Just then, she felt two fingers poking her on each side.

"Boo!" Israel shouted.

Clarisa dropped her CD to the floor. "Hey! What's the deal?"

Israel knelt down and picked up the CD. "Okay, okay, calm down. I was just kiddin' around. What's up with you?"

"Oh … oh … nothin'. I was just lookin' at the words on the back of this CD."

Israel read them. "Hmm … sounds kind of girly if you ask me."

She snatched the CD from his hands. "Well, she's my favorite singer!"

"You want me to get it for you?"

Clarisa thought. "Well … nah, that's okay. Maribel has a copy of it at home." She placed the case back on the shelf.

"You sure, babe? I got that cash from Abel." He patted his pocket.

"No, it's all right. But I am a little hungry."

"Cool. Let's go get some comida!" Arm in arm, they left the store.

As they ate at a table in the food court, Clarisa gazed around at the beautiful surroundings. The ceiling was glass, allowing the sun to beam down on them. Lush, green plants circled the maze of tables where they sat. Water trickled out of the small waterfall created in the central fountain. Momentarily, Clarisa looked at all of the people passing them.

What are they looking at? Do they know we're skipping school?

Israel took the last bite of his egg roll and asked Clarisa if she wanted to go look at some clothes. Immediately, she was ready to get up and start walking. She thought it might be a good idea to get out the food court and into a smaller place with less people around. She threw away their trash, and the two of them walked into Jenny's Department Store. As they were passing the perfume department, Clarisa began to smell the sweet and spicy aromas that floated in the air around her. She turned to Israel.

"What did you want to look at?"

"I want to check out some jeans," he replied.

"I tell you what. Let me test some of the perfumes, and then I'll meet you over by the jeans in a few minutes."

Israel agreed, made his way through the web of counters, and disappeared around the corner.

All of the different shaped and colored bottles of perfume called out to Clarisa. Light gleamed though the blue, green, and yellow glass containers, forming a glittering rainbow for her delight. She approached the counter and picked up a beautiful, white bottle in the shape of a dove. The word *Tester* was taped on the front.

"Go ahead. Try it."

Startled, Clarisa looked up.

"Oh, I'm sorry. I didn't mean to scare you."

On the other side of the counter stood a beautiful, blonde-haired woman with a gorgeous smile and perfect, pearl-white teeth. Powdery white makeup and ruby red lipstick made her look like an angel.

"Here, let me spray a little on your wrist so that you can smell the fragrance on your own skin."

Taking Clarisa's wrist, she turned it so that her palm was facing upwards. After a quick spray, the woman put the perfume down, grabbed Clarisa's other wrist, and rubbed the two together.

"Now, I want you to close your eyes, put your wrist under your nose, and take a deep breath."

Clarisa shut her eyes, raised her wrist, and took a full, deep breath, taking in the full aroma.

"Oh, wow!" She sighed. "This is totally awesome!" She had never smelled an aroma so lovely in her life. The sweet, powdery fragrance reminded her of a sunny day in a garden full of flowers. Her eyes remained closed as she took another deep breath. She wished that she could buy the bottle but knew that it was very expensive and that she would never have enough money. As she slowly opened her eyes to ask the nice woman a question, she noticed that the beautiful smile and perfect teeth were gone, replaced by a horrible frown.

What is it? What did I do?

Suddenly, Clarisa felt a strong hand come down on her shoulder, grasping firmly like a clamp. Immediately, she knew that it was not Israel. As she turned, a shock of fear traveled through her entire body. It was a police officer.

Oh my God!

"Hello, young lady," he said. "Is your mother or father around here?"

Clarisa stood, petrified.

I... I can't believe this is happening.

"Ma'am," continued the policeman, "I'll ask you again. Could you please tell me where your parent is?"

Staring up at the tall, blue-uniformed man, Clarisa tried to think of an answer.

"Well, sir, uh... my, uh... my mother... she's at the food court."

The policeman put his hands on his hips. "I'd like to speak with her if you don't mind, young lady. Is there a reason that you're not in school today?"

"Yes, sir." The lie continued. "I just came back from the doctor. My mother needed to come to the mall to buy some things, so I came with her." Biting her lip, she looked at the officer, not knowing what was coming next.

The officer scratched his chin. "Why didn't she take you back to school?"

"We don't have a car, sir. We rode the bus." She forced a smile.

Scratching his head, the police officer stood there gazing down at Clarisa. "Well, young lady, why don't you take me down to the food court and introduce me to your mother. I need to speak with her for a moment."

Not knowing what to do, Clarisa turned and headed toward the entrance to the mall, followed closely by the officer.

After a few moments, Clarisa and the police officer arrived at the big fountain in the middle of the food court.

The cop examined the area, slowly gazing from one side of the mall to the other. "Okay, young lady, where is she?"

Clarisa felt silly because she was actually looking around the food court to see where her mother was sitting.

She's not here, you dummy. Why are you looking for her?

"Young lady," the officer insisted. "Where is she?"

Clarisa could hear the impatience in his voice, but what could she do? She was stuck. Busted. No hope.

She clinched her teeth. "I don't see her, sir. She must have finished eating."

"All right. That's enough. You're going to have to come with me." The officer grabbed her arm and started taking her toward the mall security station. Panicked, she shouted out.

"Wait! There she is!"

They stopped. "Where?"

"Over there!" Clarisa pointed at a woman sitting in the far corner of the food court. She had never seen this lady in her entire life.

This is the stupidest thing that I have ever done.

The officer released his grip and turned to her. "Okay, you stay here." He walked around the big fountain toward the stranger. Clarisa stood motionless.

Dumb. Dumb. Dumb.

Arriving at the woman's table, the police officer politely introduced himself and began talking to her. He pointed at Clarisa, continuing his conversation. Then the stranger looked up and stared directly into her eyes from across the food court. Confused, the woman turned back to the officer, shaking her head no.

That's it. My life is over.

Just at that moment, Israel grabbed her hand.

"Come on, let's go!" he shouted, not giving her a chance to speak. The two started running.

Clarisa breathed heavily as they sprinted down the mall. "What... what are you doing?"

He tugged on her arm. "Come on! This is our only chance!"

Clarisa did not reply. She was too scared. She couldn't think of anything else to do, so she continued to run.

The officer looked up and saw what had happened. He immediately realized his mistake.

Israel and Clarisa ran down the middle of the mall and dashed into a big appliance store.

"Shh! We're going to hide in here," he whispered.

"Where?"

Israel looked around. "Behind that big refrigerator over there!" He pointed at the large kitchen appliance in the back corner of the store. Quickly, they walked to the back, trying not to bring any attention in their direction.

Clarisa squeezed in between the back wall and the refrigerator. Israel looked around, making sure the coast was clear. He squirmed in next to her and peeked his head out.

"I want to see if he followed us."

Clarisa peeked out around the other side. Bad luck. The policeman walked through the entrance of the store. Standing like a statue with both hands on his hips, he surveyed the situation.

"Come on. Leave," whispered Israel.

"He's here!" Clarisa said with panic.

"Shh!"

He wasn't leaving. The officer walked through the store and looked at all of the various items. Washers. Dryers. Refrigerators. He even opened several items and inspected them.

"What is he doing?" Israel commented.

The policeman started heading for their aisle.

"Oh no. He's heading right for us!" Clarisa held her breath.

The officer walked right up to the large refrigerator that they were hiding behind.

No. Please. No. Don't let us get caught. Please. No. No.

The officer opened the large refrigerator and looked inside.

"Now, this is quite a piece of work," he said. "I could use something like this." He continued to admire the large appliance as he opened the different compartments and checked the ice dispenser. "Nice, very nice indeed."

Israel and Clarisa remained motionless, holding their breath.

After a few more moments, the officer finished his refrigerator inspection and closed the door, causing it to tilt back, pushing both Israel's and Clarisa's heads against the back wall.

"Ouch!" Clarisa muttered.

Uh-oh.

The officer stopped one more time, turned, and viewed the front of the appliance.

Busted!

"Guess I better go find those kids!" he said.

Slowly, the officer turned around and marched out toward the mall. He turned right and he was gone.

"Is he gone?" Israel asked.

"Yeah, he's gone."

Both released a big sigh.

"Man, I feel so ridiculous!" Clarisa covered her face with her hands.

"Why?"

"Why? Why do you think? Look at us. We're running like a couple of criminals."

Israel giggled. "I thought it was pretty tight."

"You've got to be kidding."

Israel pulled Clarisa's arm. "Come on! Let's get out of here!"

They walked toward the back exit and left the mall. The sun blinded them as they arrived at the parking lot.

"I can't believe what just happened!" Clarisa exclaimed.

"Man, that was pretty cool! We got out of it, didn't we?"

"Yeah, I guess so." Clarisa strangely felt exhilarated by the experience, but she didn't ever want to go through something like that again.

Israel sniffed her neck. "Hey, you smell pretty good. What kind of perfume did you try on?"

"Stop. That tickles!" She laughingly pushed him away. "I don't know. It was in this white bottle shaped like a dove. I didn't have enough time to find out the name."

"You want to go back and get the name before we leave?" Israel expressed amusement at his suggestion.

She elbowed him in his ribs. "Yeah, right!"

That was a close one. Maybe... maybe this wasn't such a good idea.

The sudden silence felt awkward.

What... what am I doing?

Clarisa shook her head, trying not to think about it.

"Hey... hey, Israel, do you think it is too late for me to go back to school?"

"What?" Israel chuckled at the suggestion. "Are you kiddin' me or what? It is way past lunch already."

"Oh … nah … I was … I was just kiddin' with you." Clarisa forced a fake smile.

Israel seemed satisfied with her answer.

Well, he's right. It's too late now. We'll see … I wonder what they are doing in science class today.

"Babe, come on. We need to get outta here before anyone sees us."

They quickened their steps toward the busy street.

Clarisa wiped black streaks of makeup off her face as she and Israel marched down the street back toward their neighborhood. They thought it better to start walking than to remain at the mall to wait for the bus. The cop might spot them there.

"Israel, how much farther is the next bus stop?" Clarisa asked as she fanned herself with a napkin she took from the food court.

"It's just up here. We'll be there in a couple of minutes."

"So where are we going to go? I can't go home yet. Plus, we have to pick Juanito up."

"You don't think that Maribel will pick him up?"

Maribel pick him up … now that's a trip.

Clarisa looked at Israel with a smirk. "Now, Israel, you know we can't trust her to do that on her own. Besides, she doesn't even know we're gone. We don't know if she will wait for us across the street."

"Why not? She knows the way home. She walks by herself sometimes. Just don't worry about it. Don't you think Tía Maria can keep Juanito a little extra time?"

Man … this is tough. What should I do?

"I … I don't know."

"Sure, she can," he assured her. "He's even spent the night with her a couple of times, hasn't he? Besides, if Maribel doesn't see us after school, she will figure that we walked ahead of her and then will try to meet us there."

"Yeah, I guess, but—"

"Then don't worry about it. Why do you always have to do everything? Let someone else take care of things for once. It'll be okay."

Well...I am always the person that makes most of the decisions. I'm the oldest. I should. But maybe sometimes others need to take charge.

"I...I guess. But what are we gonna do?"

Israel kicked an empty can on the sidewalk. "Well, we can hang out at Abel's place for a little while. He told us to come by."

Although she didn't particularly like Abel, Clarisa didn't see anything wrong with staying at his place for a bit. What else could go wrong?

I hope nothing else happens. What am I doing? I shouldn't have skipped school. I should have just done my time in detention. Man! I can't believe it.

They stopped at a bus stop far down the street from the mall and sat down. The sun cooked them like fried eggs. Sweat ran down their faces. Finally, the bus came.

The two sat in the back of the bus and rocked back and forth as the wheels ran over pothole after pothole.

Israel put his arm around her shoulder. "So you are cool with everything, right, babe?"

"Uh...yeah...I...I guess. Whatever. It's cool with me. Sure."

"Good."

As Clarisa continued to move forward and backward with the bus, her head slowly fell onto Israel's shoulder.

What if they come looking for us? Do they know by now? Probably. What if Mr. Rodriguez gets mad and reports us to the police?

The bus stopped at the next bus stop. Several people got on. Clarisa's eyes remained closed. She rested and thought.

What is Maribel gonna do? Will she tell? How can she tell if she really doesn't know?

Her head stayed resting on Israel's shoulder for a few more blocks. Then the bus hit one giant hole that bounced everyone up into the air at the same time.

"Hey!" Clarisa opened her eyes, a bit dazed from her short rest.

"This is our stop, Clarisa." Israel grabbed her hand, and they exited the side door.

Again at the front of the store, they walked down the street. The air-conditioning from the bus quickly wore off, and trickles of sweat began to roll down their faces again. Israel was talking to her, something about what had happened at the mall. She really wasn't paying attention but kept nodding her head every time he said something so he would think that she was listening. Thoughts raced through her mind again.

What is Maribel gonna do when she doesn't see me after school? What's she gonna tell Mamá? What is Tía Maria gonna think when I don't show up?

An ill feeling overcame her.

"Clarisa…Clarisa! Are you listening to me?" Israel asked. "I asked if you've ever been to Abel's before."

Suddenly, Clarisa came back to reality. "No. I don't remember."

They turned off of the busy street and walked into the neighborhood. After a couple of streets, they stopped.

He pointed to a house on a corner. "Well, here it is."

Although Clarisa was used to living in and seeing places that weren't too nice, Abel's house looked so bad that it scared her. The front yard was a jungle of weeds covered with bottles, paper bags, and other trash. White paint flaked off of the sides of the house, exposing dark, rotted wood. Two of the front windows were broken, and the screen door leading into the house was falling off the hinges.

Clarisa hugged herself, rubbing her hands up and down each arm. "Are you sure that he lives here?"

Israel pointed toward the house. "Yeah, he's here all right."

A small rat ran from the deep weeds in the yard, across the broken sidewalk leading to the front porch, and to the front steps, disappearing under the house. Clarisa controlled her nerves and her stomach. Timidly, she grabbed Israel's hand and walked toward the front door. Israel pulled open the screen door and proceeded inside. Clarisa was pasted to his side.

"Hey!" Israel shouted. "Fool, where are you?"

From the other room, Abel appeared. His dirty tank top t-shirt smelled of smoke and liquor.

"What's goin' on, bro?" The two did their handshake. "So how was the mall?"

Israel gave him a slap on the shoulder. "It was all right."

They all sat down on an old, brown couch, the only furniture in the living room. The house was an oven. Dust and dirt covered the rotted, wood floor throughout the living room. No lamps were present. The only light in the house came through the windows. As Clarisa gazed around, she believed that the floors and walls were moving. While Israel and Abel continued talking, her eyes adjusted to the darkness. Then what she thought she had seen became true. Bugs. The walls were alive with the movement of small creatures. More were scampering across the floor. One such bug crawled across Abel's bare foot. He did not move. Clarisa was repulsed. Then she felt something on her knee.

"Ah!" she screamed, slapping at her leg several times.

"Ouch! You slapped me!" Israel held his hand.

"Oh, I'm sorry, Israel. It was an accident." Clarisa looked away, both embarrassed and grossed out at the same time.

"She's a tough little one, isn't she, bro?" Abel commented.

"Yeah, I guess so." Israel winked at Clarisa. She didn't acknowledge it and turned away.

The boys continued to talk about things that Clarisa didn't really understand. They mentioned a meet-up place for the Gangstas. Something about the Latin something. Abel talked about going somewhere at night with a big group. Who should wear what colors. She wiped sweat away from her forehead and cheeks as the conversation of the boys continued. She didn't like it, and what little toleration she had for Abel was fading fast.

How could Israel have stayed here the past few days?

Glancing down at her watch, she noticed that it was three thirty, time to go get Juanito. Interrupting the boys' conversation, she said, "Israel, I think we should leave in few minutes to get Juanito."

Israel put his arm around her shoulder. "But I thought we were gonna pick him up a little late."

"Yeah, but I think it's better if we just go and get him now."

Abel looked at Israel. "Fool, y'all just got here. You gonna let your little lady tell you what to do?"

Clarisa shot a mean glare at Abel. "Hey! You don't tell me what to do!"

Israel was caught by surprise. "Clarisa, chill out. We're in the man's house. You can't speak to him like that."

Abel grinned as he leaned far back into the sofa. "Don't worry about it, bro. It's okay. The little lady has responsibilities. I didn't mean to get you mad, Clarisa. If you—"

At that moment, the only good window left in the living room exploded into dozens of jagged, razor-sharp pieces across the dusty floor. Clear crystals radiating with light flew through the air. Then a loud thud was heard, followed by another. Several large rocks landed on the floor. Clarisa screamed.

"Hey!" Abel shouted. He jumped up and ran toward the broken screen door. Looking outside, his expression saddened.

"Come outside, punks! Come on out!" Shouts of a familiar voice came from the front yard.

Slowly turning around, Abel looked at Israel.

"What is it, Abel? Who is it?"

"You're not gonna believe this. It's that Number Thirty-Four that we jumped at the store the other day, and he's here with about eight other guys in my front yard."

As Abel, Israel, and Clarisa looked out the screen door toward the street, their hearts began to race like a stampede of cattle. There were approximately nine boys, maybe ten. All of them wore black jeans and purple jerseys. Many donned baseball caps that were turned sideways. Others had bald heads with long, braided strands of hair that hung like tails from the back of their heads above their necks. Number Thirty-Four stood in the middle, slapping his fist into his open hand, ready for battle. His lip was purple and swollen. Both of his eyes were blackish-gray. Clarisa figured that this was a result of the fight he had been in with Israel and the gang yesterday. She trembled with fear as she clutched her wet, sweaty hands together. When Number Thirty-Four finally spoke, she felt her heart drop to her stomach.

Number Thirty-Four put his hands around his mouth and yelled toward the house. "Let's go, punks! You fools aren't gettin' out of here without answerin' to us! We don't care if you're Gangstas or not! You're goin' down just the same!"

"How did they find out where you live, fool?" asked Israel.

Abel looked between the filthy blinds toward his front yard. "I don't know, man! Maybe they followed you dudes over here."

Another rock crashed through a window.

"Hey, Gangstas! Come out and play!" More shouts came from outside. "Hey, Gangstas, let's play!"

Clarisa shook with fear. "What are we gonna do, Israel?"

For once, he didn't have a good answer for her. He looked at Abel. "What do you think, bro?"

He was on one knee now peering outside. "Man, there's too many of them. We can't go outside, but we can't hang in here either."

Now, rocks pelted the house like a hail storm. Some came through the windows, bouncing off the floor and walls. Others banged the front and sides of the house. Then a rock struck Clarisa's arm, shocking her with pain.

"Aargh!" she screamed.

Israel ran to her. "Babe, are you okay?"

More frightened than hurt, she turned to him, crying. "I want to go home, Israel! Please, get us out of here. Take me home, please." Her head buried into his chest.

"I'll get us out of here," he answered. "Don't worry. We'll get out."

Israel could see that Abel was scared too. That was a first. He had always looked so cool until now.

"Bro, we have to do something!" Israel demanded.

Abel paced across the floor. "I know! I know!"

Walking closer to the broken screen door, Abel addressed the gang. "Hey, what's up with you guys? What do you want?"

Number Thirty-Four raised his right arm. The rock throwing immediately stopped. He stepped forward.

"You know what's up! It's payback, fool! Either you come outside, or we're comin' in there!"

"Yeah," Abel tried to shout convincingly. "If you dudes do anything to me, my homeboys will pay you back double, fool!"

Clarisa peered through one of the broken, filthy windows to get a glimpse. Number Thirty-Four stood in front of the rest of the gang like a warrior.

"Like I said, either you come out and get your tail kicked, or we come in there and do it. It's up to you, fool. We know that other punk and his girl are in there with ya too. They ain't gettin' out of this either."

Abel backed away from the door and turned to Israel and Clarisa. "Listen, y'all need to get outta here."

Israel knew that he needed to protect Clarisa, so he didn't argue about staying to fight. "What about you, bro? What are you gonna do here by yourself?"

"Don't worry about me. This is what I want you to do. Go through the kitchen to the back door. Wait there. When you see me jump outta that side window over there, I want you and Clarisa to run out the back door. Jump the fence in the backyard and run through the other yard to the other block. Just run and hide, fool! Run and hide!"

Clarisa bit her fingernails. "They're gonna catch us. I know it!"

Israel looked confidently at her. "No, they won't. I told you that I'll get us out of this."

Rocks began to beat against the rundown shack again. Abel walked over to the side window. He lifted one leg and put his foot on the ledge. Then he turned his head and flashed the Gangsta sign at Israel. Israel flashed it back. After that, he let out a thunderous scream and jumped out of the window into the narrow yard along the side of his house, disappearing. The rocks stopped.

"Come on! Let's go!" Israel shouted.

Clarisa and Israel bolted out of the back door. After a few strides, they came to the backyard fence. Israel bent down and cupped both of his hands.

"Clarisa, put your foot in my hands, and I'll lift you over the top of the fence."

As she was lifted up, she got her pants leg caught on one of the prongs at the top of the fence and tumbled over to the other side. Israel quickly leaped over the fence and into the yard. After helping Clarisa up, they turned around and got a glimpse of Abel running off in the distance down the street. A sea of purple and black was running behind him as he disappeared into the neighborhood. They looked at each other. Maybe they were finally safe.

Suddenly, walking out of Abel's back door were two of the boys from the gang. One of them was Number Thirty-Four. His eyes were fixed on Israel. A crooked smile appeared out of the corner of his mouth, and his fists clinched with the anticipation of scarring both of them for life.

"I'm coming for you, fool! You ain't gettin' out of this one, and neither is your girl!" he shouted.

"Run, Clarisa!" Israel screamed as he pulled her arm. As they ran, she tried to keep up with Israel but could not. Pain shot out from her ankle. She had twisted it from the fall over the fence.

"Israel!" she cried. "I can't do it. My ankle … it hurts so bad!"

He jerked hard on her arm. "Come on! You've got to!"

Gathering all of her energy, Clarisa forced herself to run with all of her might. The pain sent electric shocks up her entire leg, but the fear of getting caught pushed her on. She hobbled with Israel around the side of a strange yard and into the street on the other side. As she turned, she could see the two predators approaching the fence.

Israel continued pulling on Clarisa's arm, making her run faster than she ever had, even with her injured ankle. Neither of them looked back, but they knew that Number Thirty-Four and the other boy were not far behind. As they scurried past all of the old, broken-down houses that lined the street, Clarisa thought about asking Israel to stop at one of them and run inside for help. But if nobody was there, they would be quickly caught by the two hoodlums. She said nothing. They continued running.

"Israel," Clarisa panted, "I...I can't run anymore. I...I feel sick...and...I can't breathe. My foot...it hurts really bad."

They both knew that they couldn't run forever, especially with Clarisa's ankle in such bad shape. For the first time, they both looked back. The two boys were rounding the corner, catching up to them.

"Come on, Clarisa!" Israel said, pulling her arm again.

They darted into a narrow, vacant alley.

Israel whispered, "I know this alley. Me and my homeboys sometimes hang out here."

They skipped over broken bottles and trash that lined the streets. Unexpectedly, they saw a garage that was open.

"In here!" Israel directed.

Inside the dark, dingy garage was an old, rusty car. He grabbed the handle and pulled up. The door opened.

"We'll hide in here." He pushed Clarisa inside, jumped in behind her, and silently closed the door. Both lay down in the seat. Dusty filth covered the interior of the car, and old springs jutted out of the ancient car seat, painfully poking them in their backs. Their chests moved up and down in fast waves as they gasped for air. Sweat poured down the sides of both their faces.

Clarisa began to softly weep. "I want to go home."

"Shh…they'll hear us," Israel whispered.

The two stayed silent and motionless. Clarisa thought the sound of her own heartbeat would give them away. A rush of thoughts came to her.

I wish I were at home. I wish I would have gone to school. How can all of this stuff be happening? It doesn't seem real. Hiding from the police. Running from gangs. How could I let all of this happen? How? I wish I were at home.

The sounds of glass being crushed under feet and trash cans being thrown to the ground were heard in the distance. Footsteps were closer now. Clarisa thought that Number Thirty-Four might have seen them turn into the alley. Their voices got closer and closer. Then there was silence. Clarisa bit her lower lip both in terror of being found and because of the throbbing pain coming from her ankle. Still, she did not make a sound. Israel slowly turned his head and looked up at the broken rearview mirror that loosely hung above them. He elbowed Clarisa. Her jaw dropped as she looked into the mirror and saw the reflection of two purple shirts coming into the garage.

Israel and Clarisa were motionless, hoping that the two boys would not find them. Silently, Israel put both of his feet against the inside of the car door, bending his knees up to his chest. The two boys were moving around in the garage, looking behind boxes and old furniture. One of the boys passed right by the car window, but he did not look inside. Clarisa shut both of her eyes tightly and held her breath. Israel tensed his legs, tightening the pressure against the car door.

"I don't see nothin,' bro," said Number Thirty-Four. "Let's check it out farther down the alley."

The other boy stumbled around. "Yeah, I don't see anything either."

Again, staring at the rearview mirror, they saw one of the boys exit the garage and continue down the alley. They couldn't believe it. Were they going to get lucky again? Clarisa hoped so. Then her hope faded as she looked up. She saw Number Thirty-Four's reflection staring at her from the broken rearview mirror of the old car.

Number Thirty-Four walked toward the car. "Fool! Come back in here! I got 'em!"

Oh, Virgin of Guadalupe, help us, please! We are dead!

Israel pushed against the car door with all his might, causing it to fly open and crash into Number Thirty-Four's legs, thrusting him into a stack of boxes. He bounced off the pile and fell to the ground. Boxes tumbled over him, covering him from head to foot.

"Let's go!" Israel grabbed Clarisa's hand and pulled her as they ran out of the garage.

The other gangster appeared at the entrance to the garage. Israel met him with a forearm to the chin. The boy fell like a load of bricks.

"Israel," Clarisa moaned, "I … I can't walk. It hurts so much!"

He picked her up and cradled her in his arms. Then he jogged with her out of the alley as fast as he could, leaving the turmoil in the distance.

As Israel left the alley and approached a street, Clarisa bounced up and down in his arms.

"We're almost outta here, babe!" He lifted her up higher in his arms.

Clarisa wept. "Ouch … it … my ankle hurts so much."

Then screeching tires were heard. From around the corner, a car appeared. It was headed right toward them.

"Oh no!" Clarisa screamed.

Israel stopped. "What the … "

The car slid to a rapid stop, leaving black tire marks in the street.

They got us. That's it. We are finally finished.

Just when Israel began to run in the opposite direction, Clarisa squeezed his arm.

"Wait … wait, Israel!"

He stopped. "But … they're gonna get us."

Clarisa smiled. "Stop, Israel! It's … it's okay … "

"What? What did you say?"

"I said … it's … it's okay. Look … it's them!"

They looked forward and saw Mr. Rodriguez and Maribel in the car.

How could this be? Thank God!

Maribel jumped from the door of the car and ran toward them.

"Look! Look! It is them! It is them! I told you!" shouted Maribel. "It's Clarisa and Israel!"

As Maribel approached them, she slowed to a stop. She gazed at them. They looked pitiful. Dirty. Injured.

"Oh my God! What … what happened to you?" Tears formed in Maribel's eyes.

"My leg … it's hurt. I can't stand the pain."

In the distance, Mr. Rodriguez was seen getting out of the car. When he caught up to them, he looked right at Israel. "Is she okay? Can you get her to the car?"

Israel paused. "Uh … yeah … yeah … we can get in the car."

Maribel walked up to Israel and yelled. "What did you do to her, Israel? What the heck happened today? Where were y'all?"

Israel pushed forward and answered nobody. Instead, he turned his attention to Clarisa. As they got to the car, he placed her inside. She sank into the backseat, crossing her arms and closing her eyes, squinting in pain.

"Man, is she gonna be okay?" asked Maribel.

"Clarisa honey, what is it?" Mr. Rodriguez examined her leg.

"My ankle. It's killing me. Gosh … I'm so glad you are here. But how—"

"Don't worry about anything. Okay, everybody sit back." Mr. Rodriguez got everyone into the car and closed the doors. "We're going to get Clarisa to a hospital and get her checked out. Then we're going to discuss all of this mess that happened today. Do all of you understand?"

They nodded in agreement, even Israel.

Suddenly, a loud bang was heard on the side of the car. They turned and saw that Abel's face was being pushed against the side window. Clarisa screamed.

Number Thirty-Four held Abel's arm behind his back as he pushed him forward, pressing him harder against the car.

"Argh!" Abel screamed as his chin was held firmly against the driver's side car window.

Several other gang members stood behind as they evilly grinned at the horrid sight.

Clarisa buried her head in her arms. "Please, let's go. No more. No more."

Israel held Clarisa tight but said nothing. Maribel was equally silent.

Mr. Rodriguez looked at everyone calmly. "Guys, don't worry. This is going to stop, and it will stop now."

He turned to his car window and tapped on the side. Abel's face continued to be pushed flat. Again, Mr. Rodriguez tapped on the window and motioned with his hand that he wanted to roll the window down.

Number Thirty-Four looked, stopped, and threw Abel back to the rest of the gang. A sea of purple grabbed him and made him stand silently with them.

Israel sat up. "Hey, Mr. Rodriguez, that's my home-boy. We gotta get out and help him."

Mr. Rodriguez turned to him. "Israel, quiet! Let me handle this."

"Man, I ain't gonna let that dude—"

Maribel cut Israel off. "Shut up! You got everyone in enough trouble today!"

"Hey, this ain't none of your—"

Just then, Clarisa squeezed his hand. "Babe, please, hold me. Just hold me."

The car was silent. Mr. Rodriguez rolled the window down. Number Thirty-Four stepped back and crossed his arms.

Mr. Rodriguez smiled. "Boys, you don't really want to do this, do you?"

"Do what, old man?" Number Thirty-Four grinned.

Mr. Rodriguez briefly looked at the gang in the background and then stared into Number Thirty-Four's eyes.

Be careful, Mr. Rodriguez. These guys mean business.

"Gentlemen, I don't want any trouble here. The people in this car are coming with me for now. Just leave, and there won't be any problems."

"What…who you think you're talkin' to?" Number Thirty-Four clinched his fists. Several members of his gang approached the car.

Mr. Rodriguez remained calm.

"Son, like I said, these kids are coming with me. Back away from my car."

Clarisa trembled as she saw that the gang was about to open the car door. Then they stopped.

Why?

They seemed to recognize him. The boys stood and looked at each other, apparently not knowing exactly how to react.

One boy in the back stepped forward.

"Hey, we need to talk to that dude in the backseat. Tell him to get out!"

Mr. Rodriguez put both arms on the inside of the car door and looked directly up at all of them and smiled.

"Those of you that remember me from class are good kids. I know it. Don't try to do something that is going to get you in a lot of trouble. Just step back and let us be on our way."

One of the unfamiliar gang members kicked rocks toward the car, pelting the tire. "Hey, man! You can't tell us what to do! Nobody's at school right now! You're in our barrio!"

"I'm not telling anyone what to do, and this is my barrio too. I've been here since I was a kid. Don't forget that. You boys know this."

Clarisa looked at Maribel through her fingers that covered her face. She sat as close to Mr. Rodriguez as she could get in order to see every bit of the action. Clarisa tapped Israel's leg to get his attention, but he was intently listening to the conversation.

Number Thirty-Four stepped back to the window and leaned down.

"Okay, old man, I'll give you that. You've been here for a while. So what? That don't mean nothin.'"

Calmly, he put his hand on Number Thirty-Four's forearm. "I'm just asking everyone to calm down. Step back and walk away. Please do the right thing and let us drive away from here peacefully. Please."

Number Thirty-Four stood and turned around. Quickly, he formed a small circle with the other gang members. They spoke in low voices and looked back toward the car several times. Clarisa looked over the group toward the boys behind them. There, Abel still stood with two large gang members holding his arms. She focused again toward the circle of gang members. Finally, Number Thirty-Four walked back to the car.

"Okay, you can go." He turned to Israel and pointed at him. "But dude, we ain't finished with this. We'll see you again!"

Israel broke his silence. "Whatever, dude! I'll have backup with me!"

Mr. Rodriguez turned to him quickly. "Israel, shut up!"

Clarisa's eyes widened with shock. Surprisingly, Israel said nothing.

Number Thirty-Four stood, turned, and began to walk away. The others followed.

"Hey!" Mr. Rodriguez shouted. "What about him?" He pointed at Abel.

Number Thirty-Four smirked angrily. "Sorry, guys, we ain't done with that dude yet."

Hearing this, Abel shouted, "Israel! Dude! Don't worry! I'll—"

Just then, one of the gang members hit him in the stomach. Abel hunched over in pain. Now he was silent.

"Like I said, we ain't done with this." Number Thirty-Four walked back to his homeboys.

Clarisa and Israel saw Abel in the distance. For the first time, Clarisa thought she saw fear in his eyes.

Then, in unison, the gang turned their backs and slowly walked away, never glancing back toward Mr. Rodriguez or anyone else. Everyone sighed in relief.

Man, what is gonna happen to him?

Mr. Rodriguez put the car into drive. "Let's go."

THE HOSPITAL

The four of them sat in the emergency room of the hospital. As Mr. Rodriguez spoke on the phone to Señora Sanchez, Maribel watched the small television up in the corner of the busy waiting room. Exhausted from the experiences of the day, Clarisa and Israel slumped down in the tiny emergency room chairs. The area was at capacity. An old man lay next to them, snoring as if he were at home. Across from them, three young girls were standing in the corner, leaning on the wall, half-asleep. There was no other space to lay, sit, or stand.

Israel turned to Clarisa. "Hey, babe, I'm gonna go get a drink of water. You want me to bring you a glass?"

She rubbed her swollen ankle. "No, I'm all right."

"How is it?" Israel asked.

"It hurts a lot."

"Well, they'll fix you up here. Don't worry. And I promise, the dudes that did this are gonna pay, big time!"

Disgusted, Clarisa closed her eyes.

"I'll be back in a minute." Israel walked across the busy room.

I can't believe he still wants to fight after all this!

She gazed across the hectic waiting area, oblivious to the noise and movement.

Man, I'm glad they found us. But how… how did they know where we were?

Clarisa turned to Maribel and tapped her on the arm. "Hey, how did you guys—"

Maribel pushed her arm away and stared at the TV. "Shhh, this is my favorite Mexican soap opera."

Clarisa grabbed her arm with both hands. "Come on, Maribel. I need to talk to you."

Maribel pointed at the TV. "Man, hold on, she's about to tell that cowboy dude that it was her twin sister that stole the saddle and not her."

Frustrated, Clarisa jerked on her arm. "Maribel!"

Maribel turned and faced her. "Okay, okay, what is it?"

"Why did you snitch on me and Israel?"

"What?" Maribel acted as if she were accused of a crime. "I didn't snitch! You know I wouldn't do that!"

"Then how did Mr. Rodriguez find out?"

Maribel looked at her. "I don't know. This morning we both saw you and Israel walk off, but I just figured you might have dropped something. That's what I told him. Then we both went in. After school, he told me that you were absent and asked if I would go with him to look for you. But man, I never thought that you would skip.

Who would ever think you would do that? Man, I guess that there's a first time for everything. We went by the store, the pizza place, the apartments, everywhere. But we couldn't find y'all anywhere. Mr. Rodriguez wanted to go by the house, but I told him that you wouldn't be there. See, I was protectin' you. Anyway, when we were drivin,' we passed you guys up and saw y'all runnin' away from some dudes. That's how we found you."

Clarisa shook her head. "Yeah, that was pretty messed up."

"So what happened? How did all this mess start?" Maribel rubbed her hands together, waiting for a good story.

"Look, today was no joke. It was dangerous and messed up. You see—"

Just as she was about to go into the story, Mr. Rodriguez walked up to them.

"Aw, man." Maribel turned back toward the TV.

He stood in front of them.

"Clarisa, I called your mother. She will be up here as soon as she can. She has to go pick up your little brother first."

Dang it! We forgot to get Juanito. Mamá is gonna kill me.

Mr. Rodriguez knelt down. "Are you okay?"

Clarisa tried to lift her leg but sat it back down. "Yeah, my foot hurts, but I'm okay."

"I'm so glad you are going to be all right." He smiled.

Clarisa sat up. "Mr. Rodriguez, how did you find us? Who told you that—"

"Not now, Clarisa. Not now. Let's get you in to see the doctor first, and then we will talk."

Israel came back from the water fountain, paused, looked at Mr. Rodriguez, and said nothing. He sat down.

They waited in silence and watched the people walk in and out of the emergency room doors, up and down the crowded hallway.

A nurse walked out into the packed space in front of the main desk. "Clarisa Sanchez … Clarisa Sanchez … we have a room."

Mr. Rodriguez stared out the window of the hospital room, looking outside into the neighborhood. Maribel was next to him, leaning back in a chair with her eyes closed. Israel stood next to the hospital bed.

Clarisa looked at her ankle as she was lying on her back on the hospital bed. The brown bandage that wrapped around her foot was so tight that she could not feel her toes. Although the foot felt much better, her conscience did not.

How could I let all of this happen? Why did I do it?

The thoughts continued racing through her mind.

We really could have been hurt today, really bad. What was I thinking? I can't believe that I let myself get into this mess! Police. Gangs. Lies. We could have been arrested, hurt, or even killed.

The nurse entered the room and walked up to Clarisa. Everyone stopped what they were doing and listened attentively.

"Young lady, the X-rays were negative. You have a severe sprain, but you should be okay in a few weeks." The nurse rubbed Clarisa's hair and touched her cheek.

"You are fine. I will be back in a bit." She turned around and exited the room.

A sigh of relief came from everyone.

"Clarisa, the nurse said you're gonna be okay!" Maribel leaned over the bed to hug her big sister.

Clarisa looked over Maribel's shoulder and saw Mr. Rodriguez standing behind her. Her arm reached out with an open palm toward him. He stepped forward and held her hand. Israel stepped back.

"Mr. Rodriguez, thank you so much. I don't know what we would have done if you hadn't shown up," she said as tears clouded her eyes.

"The important thing is that you are safe," Mr. Rodriguez said, attempting to comfort her.

Maribel stared furiously at Israel as he continued to stand next to Clarisa, silent. Just before she opened her mouth to bark out her complaint, Mr. Rodriguez reached for her arm and slowly pulled her back. Noticing the tension in the room, Clarisa spoke.

"Maribel, Mr. Rodriguez, could you two step outside for a minute? I want to talk to Israel alone."

Maribel continued to glare at Israel, not moving.

"Maribel, just wait outside. I'll talk to you later. Please."

"Come on, Maribel," Mr. Rodriguez said, tugging on her arm. "Let's go outside like she's asking. Your mother should be coming any moment."

"Well ... okay, but remember, I want the whole story of what happened today." Mr. Rodriguez pulled on Maribel, and they walked out of the room.

Israel walked up to Clarisa and took her hand.

"Babe," he began, "I'm so glad you're okay. Man, I don't know what I would've done if somethin' woulda happened to ya."

"Well, we're both okay. That's the important thing." Clarisa caressed Israel's hand.

"Yeah, you're right."

"I feel so dumb, Israel. None of this should've happened. I should've just gone to school and went to detention. What was I thinking?"

"Hey, don't talk like that, Clarisa. You ain't dumb. You're the smartest person I know."

Clarisa's perfect smile brightened the room. "You're sweet."

"Mr. Rodriguez said your mom will be here in a few minutes. What're ya gonna tell her?"

"I don't know. I haven't even thought about it. Boy, is she gonna be upset with us."

"Well, you can tell her that she don't have to worry about nothin' anymore. I'm gonna make sure of it."

Clarisa's smile disappeared, and concern overcame her.

"What … what do you mean, Israel?"

"I mean that I'm gonna make sure that we don't have to worry about those guys no more. After what they did today, they're gonna get it bad. I gotta find out what happened to Abel."

A sick feeling arose in Clarisa's stomach as she continued to listen to Israel talk.

"I mean, can you believe it? They tried to kill us!"

His rage grew the more he talked.

"What do they think, coming to Abel's house, bustin' up his place, hitting us with rocks, chasin' us down the street like we're dirty dogs or somethin'! Man, they're gonna get theirs!"

"Israel…" Clarisa sobbed as she covered her eyes with both hands. "Stop. I can't listen to you talk like this."

Not hearing her, he continued ranting.

"Yeah, and it's gonna go down tonight! I'm gettin' ready to talk to the homeboys. They picked the wrong dude to mess with. The Gangstas are gonna hit 'em strong!"

"Enough!" Clarisa screamed.

Her shout shocked Israel to silence.

"That's enough, Israel! I don't want to hear any more of this junk!"

"Babe, what… what do you mean?"

"I mean, hasn't enough happened today? Do you want to make it worse?"

"What do you mean make it worse? What do you want us to do? Nothing? You know we can't do that. That's not how it is around here. We gotta stand up to 'em! They'll think we're punks if we don't!"

Is that how things are? Does everything really have to be like this?

"Israel, listen to me. I don't want you to go looking for those boys anymore. Just leave them alone."

"But Clarisa…"

"Israel, listen to me. Please. Everything that happened today was my fault. I should have gone to school, but I didn't. I chose to skip school. You didn't make me do it. It was my choice, a really bad choice. The stuff that happened in the mall was just plain ridiculous. We shouldn't have been there in the first place."

"Yeah, but…"

Clarisa continued. "Then going to Abel's house was really dumb. I should've just gone to Tía Maria's to pick up Juanito. You see, I should know better. I should know better than to skip school and roam the streets. I made some dumb decisions today."

"Clarisa, it wasn't your fault that those guys tried to jump us. You didn't tell them to do that. That's why I gotta do somethin' so it won't happen again."

"Israel, don't you see?" she pleaded. "Don't you see what you're doing?"

He stood perplexed.

"You aren't changing anything, Israel." She released his hand and turned her head toward the opposite wall, looking away from him. "I've always accepted things as they are, and I've always accepted you too. But things have to change. They have to change in a big way."

"What do you mean?" he asked.

"I mean, I'm not sure of this gang stuff anymore. I know the Gangstas have been around a long time, and a lot of them are cool. You know that some of them are my friends at school too. Some of their sisters and girlfriends are in my classes. But I don't think it's for me anymore. All I see is fights and everything getting all messed up."

She looked back at him.

"You told me that it wasn't my fault that those guys have been messin' with us. Maybe you're right. But it has been my choice to hang around the Gangstas and their friends. So maybe … maybe it is partly my fault."

Israel pushed his hands hard into his pockets. "What are you sayin'? 'Cause of me all of this happened?"

"No, I'm not saying that it is all your fault, but part of it is. All this fighting you do is just getting worse and worse. Pretty soon, somebody's gonna end up dead! It almost happened today! Maybe Abel is dead!"

"Don't say that."

"Well, it's true."

"So what do I do? Just let it go?"

Clarisa paused to get her words exactly as she wanted to say them.

"What I'm saying is that I don't want to be involved in it anymore, Israel. If someone is in a gang, then I'm not gonna have anything to do with them. I have to do it. If not for my sake, then for my family. You should think about it too. Just look at what you're planning. You're gonna fight again, tonight! Who knows if you'll come out of it okay this time?"

"Hey, are you telling me to ditch my homies? I hope not. You know that I could never do that!"

Now crying, Clarisa continued. "Well, I'm not telling you to do anything! I'm just telling you my choice, and my choice is not to hang out with the gang anymore!" She took a deep breath. "And if you're gonna keep fighting and hanging out with your homeboys, and they're more important to you than I am, and you're gonna keep fighting, then I don't think that we should be together anymore."

Israel couldn't believe it. "What do you mean? You're gonna break up with me just because I want to protect you?"

"You just don't get it, do you? You're not protecting anyone. All you're doing is hurting people! Until you see that, then I can't see us being together."

"But babe…"

Clarisa stared at him. "I…I just don't know, Israel. I…I just don't know."

Confused, Israel stepped back. He stood in the middle of the room, staring silently at her. Clarisa looked into his eyes. Slow tears started to fall.

The door slowly opened. Mr. Rodriguez poked his head in. He saw Israel standing silent while Clarisa quietly sobbed in her bed. He stepped in and walked slowly to Israel's side.

"Son, we need to talk."

Israel looked down and stood motionless. Clarisa continued to stare at him.

"Son, please. I'm not here to tell you what to do. Can't you see that I want to help? You know me, Israel. You know that I want to help. Deep down, you do."

Clarisa turned toward the wall and lay silently, pretending to sleep. However, she listened to every word.

"Man, it looks like I really messed up, didn't I?" he said to Mr. Rodriguez.

Messed up? Maybe he is starting to listen.

The two walked over to the window and stared outside into the parking lot. Mr. Rodriguez put his arm on his shoulder.

"Things are okay now, son. We will make everything right. Don't worry."

"Well," Israel paused, "I guess you did help us a lot. You're all right for a teacher, I guess."

Mr. Rodriguez chuckled. "I guess that's supposed to be a compliment. I'll take it."

"I never thought things were gonna get this messed up," Israel continued. "I mean, I'd never do anything to Clarisa to get her in trouble or hurt."

Clarisa smiled.

Mr. Rodriguez removed his arm from Israel's shoulder and faced him. "Israel, do you want to tell me what happened?"

"Man, so much has happened the past few days. I don't know where to start. You know, it might be better if Clarisa tells you. She's better at explaining stuff than I am. Besides, I gotta go take care of some business."

Oh no...please, please listen to him, Israel. I'm begging you.

"Israel, you know, I've lived in this neighborhood all of my life. My parents live down that street over there," he said as he pointed through the window and across the parking lot.

"Yeah," Israel replied, "I remember you saying that in class one time."

"Well, it's nice to know that you were listening to me once in a while at school."

"Your class was okay. Not too boring."

Mr. Rodriguez laughed again and was glad that he finally had his complete attention. "You know, when I was your age, I ran around with a group of kids. We ran around the streets and had places that we claimed as ours. I guess it was like a gang, but not like the ones that are around here now."

"Hey, that's tight," Israel said, very interested. "Did you dudes have a name?"

"Like I said, it wasn't like gangs are now," he continued. "Anyway, we still did a lot of the same things that y'all do now. We backed each other up when there was trouble. Sometimes we started trouble and even fought other groups. That's how it was."

"Yeah, I know what you mean," Israel replied.

Where is this conversation going?

"Anyway, none of it was any good. It eventually got out of hand. We would fight kids. Then they would fight us. One of us would get jumped, and we would jump a couple of their guys. Eventually, it got personal. I had a fight a long time ago with this kid. I didn't know him, but I knew that his friends weren't my friends. I hit him for no reason. I thought it felt pretty good hitting this kid. Was that dumb or what?"

Clarisa peeked over and saw that Israel's eyes and attention were focused on every word. She turned back around.

Come on, Mr. Rodriguez, keep him listening.

"After a few weeks," he continued, "I forgot about this kid. Then one day, my little sister, nine years old, comes home crying. Let me tell you what that kid and his friends did to her. They found out that she was my sister, followed her home from school one day, and took her to this abandoned house and locked her in. They left her there alone for hours."

Oh my goodness!

"Oh man," said Israel. "That ain't right! What did y'all do?"

"Luckily, some lady was walking by the old house and heard that little girl crying. She got her out of there. My little sister was afraid to leave our house for days after that. That's when I decided that it was over. I was getting out."

"Well, that's too bad for you. But I ain't got no family, and me and my homies are different," Israel said, standing up straight.

"Israel, I don't know what you're planning on doing, but I want you to think real hard before you do it. Right now, you're not in school. Your girlfriend is in the hospital. We don't know what happened to Abel. If this is what your gang is doing for you, then I can tell you this. They aren't doing much except helping you get into more trouble. Think about it."

Please, babe, think about what he is saying.

With those words, Israel stepped back. He turned back to look at Clarisa. She was lying on her back with her eyes closed.

He looked at her. "I don't know, man … I just don't know."

Israel reached out and shook Mr. Rodriguez's hand.

"Thanks, Mr. R. Thanks for helping. It looks like you got it under control now. I'm gonna take off before Señora Sanchez gets here. She's gonna be mad at me."

"Israel, I can talk to her. Don't worry."

"Naw, Mr. R., that's okay. I'm just gonna go. I'll check with you guys later."

He looked at Clarisa but did not say anything. As Israel approached the door and opened it, he turned around.

"Thanks again, Mr. R. You are cool." He turned and walked out.

Immediately, Clarisa opened her eyes. "Do you think he listened?"

"We'll see, Clarisa. We'll see."

A moment later, Señora Sanchez bolted through the door with Juanito in her arm. Maribel jogged in behind her.

"Clarisa, mi hijita! What happened?"

"Mamá … oh, Mamá."

They embraced.

BACK AT SCHOOL

The next afternoon, Clarisa and Señora Sanchez arrived at the school to speak to the principal. Still trying to get used to the crutches that the hospital had given her, she slowly hopped through the school doors and into the front office. Nervously, she flopped down into one of the chairs. Señora Sanchez sat down next to her.

What a mess I made. What is going to happen to me? Why did I do this? Too late now. Have to accept the consequences, whatever they are.

After a few moments, the secretary approached them. "Clarisa, the principal will see you two now."

Her heart thumped against her chest. "Okay."

The principal greeted them at they entered his office. Señora Sanchez helped Clarisa sit down. Then the meeting began.

"Thank you for coming to school on such short notice, Miss Sanchez," the principal began. "It shows how much you care for your children."

"Oh, yes, sir! My children are the most important things in my life."

"Yes, ma'am, I can see that." Pausing briefly, he turned toward Clarisa. "Clarisa, Mr. Rodriguez came to me this morning and told me quite a story about what happened yesterday. You had quite an experience."

"Yes, sir. It was an experience that I want to forget. And sir, I am sorry for skipping school yesterday. It was very wrong to do that."

"Yes, Clarisa, you are right. That was a very poor choice. But we're not here to talk only about that. There is something else I want to tell you."

"Sir?"

"Clarisa, you are a very bright, charming, and dedicated young lady. Mr. Rodriguez and the rest of your teachers speak very highly of you. And although you may have made a few mistakes over the past few days, there have been far greater mistakes made by this school."

What? Where is he going with this?

"Clarisa, on behalf of Juarez Middle School, I would like to apologize to you."

The principal is apologizing to me? I can't believe it! Why?

"You see, Clarisa," he continued, "Mr. Rodriguez, a man that I greatly admire because of his dedication to the children at this school, explained everything to me. He not only told me about yesterday's happenings but also about you. All the things that you do for your family are very commendable. You have a great responsibility and do a great job at home."

Señora Sanchez beamed with pride upon hearing these words. Clarisa was still speechless.

"We are sorry for not doing a better job of listening to you. He told me that the two of you spoke at the hospital yesterday with your mother and that you told them everything that happened yesterday. He also said that he did not give you a chance to tell him what had happened at the apartments the other morning before he sent you to the office. I am afraid that we did not do a good job in the front office of listening to you either. Clarisa, we let you down, and I am truly sorry for that. Will you accept our apology?"

The school apologizing to me. Isn't that something.

"Sir, I really don't know what to say. I mean, look at everything that has happened. It's all my fault."

"No, it isn't," Mr. Rodriguez added. "If I may, sir?"

The principal nodded with approval.

"The fault lies with many different people. Sure, you made some mistakes, but the school made the biggest mistake of all. We didn't listen. You, as well as all students here, should know that the teachers and principals need to listen when there is a problem." Mr. Rodriguez looked at the principal.

"Yes, he is right, Clarisa," the principal agreed. "All I can say is that we will try our hardest not to let it happen again. Adults are not perfect. We make mistakes also. Do you accept our apology?"

Clarisa did not know how to answer, so she just sat there speechless. Señora Sanchez nudged her with her elbow.

"Yes … uh … yes, sir," she finally said. "I … I do accept the apology."

This feels so weird.

"Good. I am so pleased. Now, let's see here. We have accepted our part of the blame, and it seems that you recognize that you also made some inappropriate choices, namely, skipping school."

Clarisa covered her face with her hands. "Oh yes, sir. That was the dumbest thing that I've ever done."

Smiling, the principal continued. "Well, I think that one day of detention on Monday should about do it. Don't you think?"

Excited, she sat up straight. "Oh yes, sir! Yes, sir! You bet I'll be there! I won't say a word either! Just watch, I'll—"

"Okay, okay." The principal chuckled. "I will see you here Monday morning."

"Yes, sir. Thank you."

Clarisa rose and hobbled out of the meeting on her crutches with her mother following closely behind her. Mr. Rodriguez approached them in the hallway.

"Uh, Clarisa, may I speak to you for a moment?" Mr. Rodriguez asked.

"You go ahead, hijita. I'll wait for you outside in the front of school." Señora Sanchez kissed her on the cheek and walked out of the front doors.

The two sat down on a bench in the hallway.

"Clarisa, I wanted to know if you have heard from Israel."

"No," she sadly replied. "I haven't heard from him. Why do you ask?"

"I just wanted to know if he got in any more trouble last night."

She frowned. "No, he hasn't come by or anything. So ... I don't know."

Mr. Rodriguez held her arm. "The word from Maribel at lunch today was promising. She said that nobody had told her anything during school today and that she would have been one of the first ones to know if anything had happened with Israel."

Clarisa laughed. "Well, she's probably right. She would know. Gosh, that makes me feel better."

"I'm glad to hear that. Maybe everything will work out after all."

Clarisa grabbed his hand. "I hope so."

"I hope so too. You had better go outside and meet your mother."

"Okay."

Clarisa got up and slowly hopped to the front doors of the school on her crutches. Then she turned around.

"And Mr. Rodriguez ... "

"Yes, Clarisa?"

"Thank you again. You are a great teacher and a good friend."

Mr. Rodriguez fought back tears of happiness.

"Thank you, Clarisa. You are a great student and a good friend too."

She turned, hopped outside, and left school.

THE QUINCEAÑERA

Several weeks passed quickly, and Clarisa's birthday arrived. A quinceañera was the biggest celebration a family had, besides a wedding. The church celebration was everything that Clarisa had dreamed about and more. Stunning pink roses lined the aisles and walls, filling the air with their sweet fragrance. Her elegant pink dress cascaded behind her as Maribel followed her up to the altar, tending the delicate fabric as it trailed behind her. As she stood there, the touching church readings and lovely music filled her with such happiness that she felt like she was floating, as she had in her dreams.

At the end of the ceremony, a thunderous roar of cheers and clapping came from her many friends and family members who were present. She walked down the aisle toward the front doors of the church, followed by Maribel and an organized line of her best friends, all dressed almost as beautiful as she. She turned, smiled, and waved at the many friends and family that stood and clapped for her from the benches in the church.

That evening, the festivities continued in the church hall. All of the flowers from the ceremony were brought to the dance and surrounded the dance floor. A huge white birthday cake with four different tiers stood at one side of the hall, along with a small cake for Maribel, who would be celebrating her fifteenth birthday the following year. All entered the hall in their most elegant clothes, waiting patiently in line to be greeted by Clarisa, the woman of honor for the evening. Following a few words and tears from Señora Sanchez, the lights dimmed, and the dancing began.

Maribel was the life of the party, as usual. She could not be kept off the dance floor. Neither could Mr. Rodriguez, who danced with Señora Sanchez, Maribel, and even Juanito. After a couple of hours, the lights came back on, and the cake was cut. More cheers and whistles followed. Finally, toward the end of the night, some of Clarisa's favorite songs were played. One by one, many of the boys asked Clarisa to dance. She danced a few times, but then her mood began to sadden. Returning to her seat at the main table, she gazed around at all the guests who were eating, dancing, and singing.

This is all so great. I should not be sad. But I miss him so much. I miss Israel.

She looked down into her plate of cake.

Man, it has been almost a month already. Where is he? Why hasn't he called? Why hasn't he come back to school yet?

She picked at her cake with a fork.

He knew it was today.

All of her friends from school were dancing and having a great time. It almost looked like half the school showed up. Lines formed in front of her table as friends and families passed, giving her presents and kisses on the cheek. For a moment, she hid her sadness and acknowledged all of the well-wishers.

Other boys continued to ask her to dance, but she turned them all down.

Oh well… I can't just sit here the rest of the night. Everyone is gonna think something is up.

Then she felt a tap on her shoulder.

"Would you like to dance?" the boy asked.

He was dressed in a blue suit and even wore a tie.

Clarisa jumped. "Israel! I … you … you look great!"

"You still didn't answer me. Do you want to dance or not? Is your foot okay now?"

"Uh … yeah. Sure. My foot is fine now. Been off crutches for a week."

The two rose and entered the crowd just as a soft, slow melody began. Clarisa did not know where to start.

Israel pulled her close, and they began to dance cheek to cheek. Across the floor, Clarisa saw Maribel and Señora Sanchez looking at them. At first, they did nothing. Then she saw them smiling.

"Hey, Clarisa, this is your night. I don't want you to feel funny dancin' with me or nothin'. Just to let you know, I've been okay."

"Oh, Israel," Clarisa sighed. "I'm so happy to hear that."

They continued dancing without talking for a few moments.

"Clarisa, I just want you to know that I listened to what you told me at the hospital, and I'm tryin' to change some things. I'm not sayin' that everything is perfect, but I am changing some stuff."

"Like what?"

"Well, I'm startin' back at school next week. That's one thing."

Clarisa squeezed him tighter. "Israel, that's great!"

"Yeah, I'm gonna give it a try. Plus, me and Abel aren't talkin' no more."

"Why? What happened?"

"Well, after he got outta the hospital, let's just say that we don't see eye to eye no more. But that's enough about me. This is your night. I just wanted to stop by and tell you how much you mean to me."

"Oh, Israel, you mean so much to me too. I missed you so much!"

The song ended. Israel slowly stepped away from her, holding both of her hands.

"I'm gonna go now."

Quickly, she stepped to him. "Israel, you don't have to leave. Let's go talk to Mamá and Maribel."

He smiled. "No, not tonight. Maybe I'll come over in a few days. I'll talk to your mom then. I have a lot of explaining to do."

Taking her hand, he walked her back to her table. He leaned down and politely kissed her on the cheek. Then he stood.

"Happy birthday. This is your night. Remember, you are now a beautiful woman!"

Clarisa gazed into his romantic, dark eyes. He slowly turned and disappeared through the crowd toward the exit, like a fading dream.

Maybe it can work out after all. Maybe.

The party at the church hall lasted well into the early morning hours. Friends and family asked Clarisa to dance. She did. Seeing Israel brought up her spirits. Just knowing that he was okay thrilled her. After the dance, a few guests continued the party at the Sanchez apartment, where more food and fun awaited them. Eventually, the guests began to leave. Mr. Rodriguez finally said his good-byes at the end of the night.

"I'll see you at school, Clarisa," he said.

Clarisa waved. "Okay, good night, Mr. Rodriguez."

The girls helped their mother clean the apartment and got ready for bed. Clarisa brought Juanito to his crib from the living room, where he had fallen asleep. Maribel was on the mattress on the floor.

Clarisa motioned for her to get up. "Maribel, tonight is your night for the bed."

"I know, but it's your special night. You can have it."

"Hey, I never knew you could be so sweet." Clarisa laughed as she turned off the lamp and got into bed.

"Yeah, just don't get too used to it, big sister. I don't want everyone thinkin' I've gone all nice or something."

"No." Clarisa laughed. "I wouldn't want you to have a good reputation or anything."

"Hey, wasn't tonight great?"

"Yeah." Clarisa smiled. "It was perfect. It was the best day of my life."

"I hope my birthday next year will be like yours." Maribel pulled the covers up.

"It will be. It'll be the best. You'll see."

"Man! I can't wait!" She closed her eyes and smiled.

"Good night, Maribel."

As Clarisa lay in bed, the soft glow of the moonlight shined through the window and onto the bedroom door. The poster of the Virgin of Guadalupe was gently glistening, making her seem almost alive, like an angel.

"I guess someone has been watching over me after all," Clarisa said to herself as she closed her eyes and waited for dreams to come. And finally she did dream.

She was dancing with Israel again. Everyone in the room smiled and clapped for them as they turned around and around, elegantly stepping to the wonderful music.

"Israel, this quinceañera is so great. Thank you for being here." Clarisa danced on her toes like a ballerina.

"Yes, it is great! You are great!" He moved next to her in perfect rhythm.

As she continued to dance with him, she felt him step away. For a moment she was by herself. Then loud roars and claps from her friends and family came forth as someone else stepped in to take Israel's place on the dance floor. She held the man close as they turned and floated in the middle of the dance floor. The church hall roof opened, and the stars once again twinkled above them. Out of the corner of her eye, she saw Israel standing on the side of the dance floor, smiling and clapping for her.

"Happy birthday, hijita. I hope that you had a special day," the man dancing with her whispered into her ear.

"Oh, it was great! Thank you. Thank you so much."

"You had a special day. You are so wonderful. I am so proud of you. I love you!"

"I love...I love you too...Papi! Thank you for coming."

Clarisa slept peacefully.

She smiled.

ABOUT THE AUTHOR

Craig S. Mullenix, Ed.D., is a teacher, principal, and university professor in Houston, Texas. He grew up in the largely Hispanic community on the near north side of the city. He has traveled extensively throughout Mexico and greatly enjoys his life as a father and a husband. He wholly supports the Mexican-American community in which he was raised and is an advocate for the Hispanic community and autism awareness.